EVERYONE HAS A STORY

Everyone Has A Story

PHIL POCHUREK

LUMINARE PRESS
WWW.LUMINAREPRESS.COM

Everyone Has A Story
Copyright © 2022 by Phil Pochurek

All rights reserved. This book or any portion thereof may not be reproduced or used in any manner whatsoever without the express written permission of the publisher, except for the use of brief quotations in a book review.

Printed in the United States of America

Luminare Press
442 Charnelton St.
Eugene, OR 97401
www.luminarepress.com

LCCN: 2022906043
ISBN: 978-1-64388-975-7

*...coffee and poetry in the morning
are my baking soda on the bee sting of life.*

LUNA

4/2008 – 12/21/2021

Dedication

It is with a heavy heart that I dedicate this final book in a trilogy of poems and short stories to a beautiful blue-eyed piece of my heart who chose to go home to be with her dearest friends over these Christmas Holidays. Luna, Shu Shu, Luna Belle, Doodi...was laid to rest on December 21, 2021 after thirteen years of loving duty to her family and friends.

    Our hearts are broken, heavy, and missing our favorite girl who gave our hearts an extra beat every time we came in view of her beautiful blue eyes. Her Husky conversations were the highlight of our days and nights and will be missed in the days, months, and years ahead. Thank you, Luna, for all the miles we shared and the counsel you gave me with your patient ears. Come find me, with Ruby and Joe, when it's my time to come home and take the wrinkles out of my heart, like you always did....

CONTENTS

Loose Ends 1
What We Do 3
Too Late For Forgiveness 5
At Last An Orphan 7
The Hands Of The Craftsman 9
It's Interesting 11
Life Is Short: Use The China 13
With 15
Lipstick Memories And Perfume Dreams 17
A Blessing For All Time 23
Another Season 26
Sunday Morning Lancelots 27
Clothesline Sheets 29
A Last Taste Of Summer 31
Early In The Morning Or Late At Night 33
Bella's BIG Adventure 35
Here Come The Holidays Again 63
Another December To Remember 65
Shouting Sun Whispering Moon 67
Shouting Sun and Whispering Moon 71
Furs And Purrs 75
Sweet Bones 77
My Four-Legged Heart 79
Love Without Purpose 80
The Fourth Of July Tree 81
Looking Down 93
A Road To Nowhere 95

No More	97
Pink Slips	99
In The Rain	101
The Year They Left The Lights Up	103
Love From Behind The Mask	113
Alone Together	115
A New Normal	119
Uncertain Times	121
Nut Ratz	124
Leg Love	125
A Brand New Day	127
Without Dog	129
Run To Me	135
All Things Left Behind	137
So Many People	141
The Locker Room	143
Last Night's Clothes	145
He Sings In Tongues	148
Ashes To Ashes Dust To Dust	149
Two Words	151
With Heads Bowed Low	153
A New Golden Calf	157
At 4:45	160
In Every Soul We See	161
The Old Ones	163
When The Devil Comes To Dinner	165
The Wings Around Your Heart	167
Everyone Has A Story	169

Loose Ends

The irony in life is
That it's not the knots
In our lives that hold us back,
It's the loose ends.
The unfinished business,
The words unspoken,
That's where the trouble begins.
From things left undone or broken,
Not said or never heard.
It's an open sore that never heals
Deep inside of us.
The ones no one sees,
But you can feel...
Still raw beneath the layers of years.
Just under the skin
Where the pain is real
Hidden in the quiet moments
Behind those midnight tears.

But with every new beginning
Comes a new piece of rope.
A lifeline strong and unfrayed,
A tie that binds us to this world with
Something to hold onto when things get tough
So we won't become fearful or afraid.

Don't wait till you're
At the end of your rope
Lookin' for a knot to hold onto
To keep you afloat.

And it's too late to make amends.
When you reach for that knot
To save yourself but all you come up with
Are loose ends.

What We Do

We all make our way
Down this road we call life;
Some of us go it alone
Others as husband and wife.
Becoming who we are,
Some of us will make it
To the end of the road
And some of us not so far.
No one really knows.
Our parents come together
And then we're here,
And the rest is how it goes.
We're born, we grow up,
We find our lot in life that defines us
By what we do
But it may not be who we are.
It makes it easy for us
To put a name with a face.
Makes us feel good
About ourselves or not...
And gives us a sense of place.
It may not be who we really are,
But for some
It may be all they've got.
The paths we take are just the way
To get to where we're going
But may not be what's in our heart.
But it will do until we're knowing
And the day we can tell them apart.
Remember the next time

You meet someone
And they ask you what you do;
If what you tell them
About yourself is what's
Really inside of you.

Your paintings may be beautiful,
Your poetry so sincere,
The music you make
Warms the heart and is
Pleasing to the ear...
Your family must be
So proud of you.
Oh by the way before I leave,
What was it you said
That you do?

Too Late For Forgiveness

Hurt feelings cloaked in anger
Tear and rent into a broken heart.
Too many years in the breaking.
Words spoken out of pain in haste;
Too late to take back what's been torn apart.
Too many years in the making.
Forsaking any reconciliation.
Words like cord wood thrown
Onto a fire, stoking the flames of pride.
Creating a divide
Too often,
Too large,
Too late,
To reach across to the other side
And ask for forgiveness.
A fire so hot
It burned across the years.
So deep that time itself
Couldn't heal the wound.
Embers smoldering so deep in a hurt
They never went out...
Or came to ash.

Until now.
Too bad the wood ran out
Before my pride did.
Now there's no one left on the other side
To beg forgiveness.

To tell them I'm sorry.
To reach across and make things right
Before they died.
Buried under a pile of ashes
Where a fire burned bright,
Lays a jagged scar
Across a broken heart full of regret.
Where the flames of pride burned tall.
Defeated in victory
By the prize itself...
Then cheated by death
I lost it all.

At Last An Orphan

What's left of
my sister is all over
my house now... literally.
And she's nowhere at all.
Just some of the things
she left behind at the end.
The gene we shared that
made us gather, collect
buy and store things,
hoard the things we liked
from ceiling to floor
is evident now, even more so
everywhere in this room.
In the dishes we ate on
the Thanksgiving she blew up.
When she let all of us know
how fucked up we were
before she left,
Then came back at Christmas
and finished us off.
My sister could take
Mr. Rogers Neighborhood
and turn it into "August: Osage County"
at the turn of a phrase.
But now all that's left
are some of the hard things she loved.
I saved a few of her
Sweetest possessions.
A silver brush, an antique mirror...
Our mothers watch.

The few things she owned for years.
Touched and used over her lifetime
Soften her spirit now, in my hands,
And sweeten her memory.
Only my stubbornness was harder
Than her anger was hot,
and it cost me a chance to ask
for her forgiveness at the end...forever.
And say my last farewell.
Now I'll never know
How broken her heart really was
And she will never tell.
Her ashes are all I've got.

The Hands Of The Craftsman

In the hands of the craftsman
Are the tools of his trade;
To build or repair
All things that are made.
To fix or maintain is every tools creed.
Built to perfection
Each tool has a need.
In the hands of the craftsman
The right tool will succeed.

In the hands of the craftsman
These tools did their best,
And now their work is done;
Their time has come and past.
After thousands of hours, year after year,
Now in this box with loving care,
These tools have finally come to rest.
They did their jobs when they were needed;
Met every challenge
And the craftsman succeeded.

And now at last
They're work all done
I pass these tools on to you,
One by one to hold and view.
These works of art from the art of work
And all that they've been through.

From the hands of the craftsman
With the love and respect that's due,
After all these years
They've passed the test of time.
And now I pass them on to you.

It's Interesting

It's interesting how we all change,
Adapt, adjust to the end of our routines.
Thirty, fifty, sixty years
With not much in-between.
Love and marriage, houses and farms,
Maybe even a little travel
To get us through the years; the routines
Through the same thing year after year.
Holding babies and grand babies in our arms
That reminds us why we're here and
Determines in the end how we go on;
If we make it through or we unravel
When we're done.
Sometimes I wonder if I went too fast
Or waited too long to have any fun,
And what it would look like in the end;
When we're too old to run
And it gets harder to bend.
How long are we going to last, anyway?
Maybe I should have asked God before now
What he thought I should do.
Looked up once in a while
Instead of straight ahead.
Listened a little better too.
Now that I've reached the water
I've suddenly forgotten how to swim.
Sometimes I panic and close my eyes,
And just want it all to end.
Is this what I worked so hard for?
Saved everything up until now.

When does the fun begin?
And who wants to show me how?
All questions I keep to myself
Too ashamed to ask anyone else now.
Maybe I'm the only one who feels this way.
I'll probably never know.
It's interesting what we think about
At the end of the day.
When we don't know where to go.

Life Is Short: Use The China

It was just a Friday dinner
On the table that we eat at everyday.
Our friends were coming over
After work for dinner
Who we asked to come yesterday.
So I opened a bottle of red
As you began to set the table.
And while pouring you a glass I heard you say
"Life is short let's use the china.
It's too pretty to keep hidden away.
After all these are our best friends
So this isn't just anyday."
What's the use of waiting for Christmas
When the ones we love are here today?
We may only have this moment,
Let's not let it slip away.
"Life is short let's use the china"
Is what I remember you said,
"Before this moment is gone forever
Then quietly slips away,"
And poured another glass of red.
We don't have to wait for Thanksgiving
Turkey, sweet potatoes, and pumpkin pie,
When a lifetime of holiday memories
Can be gone in the twinkling of an eye.
Only then do we realize the value of life
And how fast time comes and goes
Then passes us by....

Now every time our friends come over
We eat on our new favorite plates.
Life's is short so we use the china
Before we're gone and it's too late.

With

With
The hardening of some attitudes
And the softening of your pride.
With
Your memories
Come the platitudes
From way down deep inside
That ring out loud and true.
Do unto all others
As you would have them
All do unto you.
With
The passing of time
We may learn to see a little more
Even as our eyes begin to fade.
With
Our lips pursed shut
We may hear something new
That we haven't heard before.
With
All the changes going on
To our bodies and our minds
We still have time to pray.
Because we know that there is someone
Who cares about what we have to say.
With

Our heads bowed low
And our hands held high
This much we can always know;
We can count on the Lord to lift us up
Fill our hearts with love
And be there when we die.

Lipstick Memories And Perfume Dreams

It was the summer of 1962. Life was good when you were a boy growing up in Oregon. The summers were hot and gas was cheap. Kids played outside till dark and rode their bikes everywhere. The boys mowed lawns, delivered newspapers, and played baseball. The girls babysat and watched the boys. Life was simpler then and safer, or at least it seemed that way. Summers were carefree and fun when you were nine. Lots of camping out in backyards and sleepovers at friends' houses. That is where this particular memory was made. An eternal flame was lit in a single, innocent, loving gesture. One that would come to me throughout the whole of my life, lighting my past with its flame and warming my present with its glowing memory.

Don had a nice family. His dad was tall and worked for the Forest Service. His sister was a cutie, and I'm sure she would someday become as beautiful as her mother, but for now she was a pest. Then there was Don's mother, Carrie. She was someone you could never forget. If Don only knew the real reason for our friendship was so I could be around his mother, he would probably be laughing the whole time he was beating me up. She was the most beautiful woman I had ever been around or close to on a regular basis. Everything about her made me stupid whenever she was around. Her voice, her hair, her face and figure, everything. Especially her big brown eyes. She could melt the Popsicle right out of your hand. She was perfect, and she was so nice. I never heard her raise her voice once, for any reason. I loved being around her. Of course, impressing a nine-year-old boy in 1962 wasn't a hard thing to do. I often wondered if Don felt the same way about his mother as I did. Probably not. He was too close to her to see her like I did. I'm sure Don loved his mom; we all love our moms. The only difference was that I was in love with Don's mom or at least a nine-year-old boy's version of love. I guess at that age you would call it a crush. I loved being around her.

I've carried the memory of Carrie's perfume (Chanel No. 5, I believe) and her loving hugs with me all these years, like an old love letter folded up and protected in the wallet of my past. Occasionally, whenever I was lonely or sad, I would warm my heart with memories of her. She helped shape the physical mold for all the women in my relationships to come for some time. It took many years for me to let go, one by one, of all the requirements on her list that every girl I met had to measure up against. I retained two: lipstick and perfume. This opened up my playing field considerably, while allowing me to hold on to the smallest memories of Carrie without hurting anyone's feelings. A flower's beauty is often stunning, and though it is brief, it is glorious. And when its beauty fades, there are two things that are most remembered: its scent and its color. Later, whenever either one of these features are recalled, you can see the flower again. You may not always remember exactly what it looked like, but its color and scent you never forget. And so it was with Carrie. Her perfume and ruby red lipstick have kept her memory alive for me all these years. Just the hint of Chanel No. 5 or the sight of a pair of dark red lips passing by brings back her memory.

Carrie was Rita Hayworth, Olivia de Havilland, and Marilyn Monroe all rolled into one. I was so enamored by her, so shy whenever she was around, I thought I would burst. On this particular night, Don's mom and dad were going out to dinner and dancing at the country club. I had no idea the vision I was about to see.

It was seven thirty when Don's dad came down the hall to the living room where Don and I were eating popcorn and watching *Gunsmoke*. Don's dad (Carl, I believe) was a nice man. He was tall and dark with emerald green eyes and a deep, clear voice. The kind you hear on radio shows. He sat down with us for a minute to wait for Carrie to finish getting ready. He reminded us of the rules for the evening, told us a few jokes, and asked us to be good for Carol, their next-door neighbor, who would be watching us while they were out to dinner. The windows were open in the living room, and a light breeze was coming down the hall from Carrie's room, carrying the slightest scent of her perfume. We heard the familiar click of a woman's high heels on the hardwood floor. We all turned around in time to see Carrie step out of the hallway to say she was ready to go and to tell us good night. She was so beautiful—more than I could have ever imagined. From the tips of her spiked high heels to her ruby red lips. She knelt down and gave us each a hug so warm and fragrant I thought I was going to melt. She was gorgeous—like a movie star right in my own arms. No wonder she chuckled when she asked us how she looked and told us to be good for Carol. She smiled when she looked down at me, but my speechless face must have said it all. Don slugged me in the arm to snap me out of it as we watched them leave. Carrie had said she might see us when she came home if we were up.

Don and I sat on the front porch waving goodbye as his parents got in their car and drove off. I don't even remember the rest of the evening. It's a wonder that night made any sense at all. In fact, in later years, as Don and I grew up and our relationship changed, this one summer night stands out in all the time we spent together.

At about ten thirty or eleven o'clock, I heard a car door close in the carport. It seemed as though I had just closed my eyes when I heard the kitchen door close and soft talk between Don's parents. As I heard Don's dad walk toward their bedroom, there was a brief pause, and then the faint sound of Carrie's high heels clicking down the hall to Don's room to check on us. Moonlight flooded the room and covered us in white. As Carrie quietly entered our room, the summer breeze scented my dreams with her presence. Only I wasn't dreaming. I was awake now and waiting for this moment: for one last glimpse of this vision of beauty.

Don was asleep as Carrie tiptoed over to kiss him good night first. Even though I was able to feign being asleep, peeking through my eyelashes, I could see everything. The moonlight shifted in the breeze through the curtain just enough to help me pull it off. But when Carrie came over to my bed, I thought my heart was going to give me away. It was beating so hard, and racing so fast, surely she would be able to hear it right through my chest. The subtle smell of cigarettes and perfume lingered on her gabardine jacket as she bent over the bed to kiss me good night. She held her long brown hair back with one hand so it wouldn't hit my face and wake me up. She sat on the edge of my bed for a moment in the moonlight and watched me for what seemed like forever before she kissed me on the cheek. Her ruby red lips glistened in the moonlight. The scent of her perfume made me dizzy as I watched her. She bent over me ever so slowly, pressing her face, her lips, against my cheek, and kissed me so gently, so sweetly, as not to wake me up. I couldn't have imagined a better kiss. Her lips and cheek were so soft, so fragrant; it was like being kissed by a rose. Slowly, she sat back up and looked at me for a moment, maybe to make sure I was still asleep. Then she got up and walked out of the room and into my heart forever, as she quietly closed the door behind her. I felt like a million bucks.

The next morning I woke up a little before Don, so I went to the bathroom first, toothbrush in hand. I flicked on the light switch, and without looking up, proceeded to overload my toothbrush with toothpaste and began brushing my teeth. It wasn't until after my first rinse that I looked up into the mirror over the sink. That's when I first noticed it. On my left cheek was the faintest outline of something red. I rinsed again and rubbed my eyes to make sure I was seeing clearly. Then, upon closer inspection, I realized—or I should say I recognized—what it was. There, on my cheek, was the faintest crimson outline of the most perfect pair of the sweetest lips in the whole world. That's when I knew I wasn't dreaming about the night before. The moonlight visit by Carrie and her goodnight kiss really happened. And there on my cheek was the proof. I relished that moment in the mirror, swooning over the fact that I wasn't dreaming and that Carrie's kiss was real.

I heard Don getting up in the next room. He asked what I was doing. I knew my time with Carrie and her lipstick kiss were short. I waited until the very last moment before Don came into the bathroom before I took the soaped washcloth in my hand and began scrubbing away this loving reminder of a sweet gift to a silly kid from the night before. Don thought I was crazy: first for brushing my teeth before breakfast and second for washing my face. Then, jokingly, he called me a mama's boy. If he only knew how right he was. With one kiss on the cheek, his mother had impressed on me a mold that all other young women who came into my life would have to fit into in some form or another. It was a curse that I'm sure broke a few hearts over the years—mostly mine.

As all our lives moved on, I grew out of my infatuation with Don's mother. So many things were happening. The president of the United States was shot and killed. We landed on the moon, there was a war going on that nobody wanted or understood, and everybody watched on the six o'clock news while they ate dinner. The summers came and went much faster than they must have seemed to at the time, but soon my school days were over.

    Don's sister, Karen, grew up to be every bit as beautiful as her mother, only looking more like her father. As for Carrie, she held her beauty for many years, slowly fading into the everyday routine of motherhood. Household chores and daily errands run on coffee and cigarettes slowly took their toll on Carrie, and eventually took her life. She passed away from lung cancer when she was only forty-eight years old. Too soon for such a bright star to go out, for such a beautiful flower to fade. Before Carrie became ill, occasionally I would see her out with Karen at a baseball game or at the grocery store. And in all those years in sickness and in health, the one thing that didn't change about Carrie was her smile and those ruby red lips, her lips and a kiss that I'll never forget.

A Blessing For All Time

As I look around this gathering tonight
I realize that something BIG is about to happen!
And today is just the beginning.
Something as perfect and natural
As the sunrise in the morning
Or the tide going out at the end of the day.
Dianna and John just seem to fit together
In that same natural and beautiful way.
I can only speak of what I know
From all the things I've seen
As I've watched this young lady
Blossom and grow into this beautiful bride;
The one you see before you today,
And all the years I've known her in between
To know that God has a plan.
And we have all come here to bear witness to
The bearing of His fruit.
The joining together of Dianna in His name
With this fine young man, John,
On this long awaited day...
Who with his heart and soul has pledged
"Till death do us part in sickness and in health
For richer or poorer," all the obvious things
Of this earth and our daily lives
One can possibly give to another person
To profess their undying love,
Before God and all who are present.
Much more than anything else this earth has to offer

Is this truth... that John loves Dianna,
And Dianna loves John.
I'm sure as much as their mothers and fathers do.
Love each other enough to become flesh of their flesh
To become one in their life as they make it, build it
Going forward in the precious time
They have together, as one heart
On their journey down the road that lies ahead.
This is their love story for the ages.
To add to the book of life.
One that all who have gathered here today
Have a chapter in, and now it's their turn
To add their pages into the book
We all know too well.
To write their story together
From this day forward as one,
And ever after whatever may come,
The rest only time will tell.
Two young lives close to all of our hearts
Some who have known them
Right from the start.
Mothers and fathers, sisters and brothers,
Friends and family all gathered here today
To bear witness to this union and pray
That their years together be plenty and long.

That whatever comes their way
They be strong and true to their promise
Made on this day to love each other
And stay true to their hearts.
Let God be their judge
And show them the way,
And rain down His blessings upon them...
Forever and today.

Another Season

I see another season
Is upon us as the trees
Begin to show their colors.
And the geese sing their arias
In great sweeping vees
Across the October skies.
Though unseasonably warm
The birds know better
As they feather their nests
For the winter.
I'm always in awe and amazed
By the bright flushing colors of fall.
The trees put on as they dress down
Before they lose all their leaves
For their long winters sleep.
Quietly blushing I'm sure is their reason...
And realize how blessed I am
To have come around with them
To bear witness to this glorious event.
One more time in my life for
Another season.

Sunday Morning Lancelots

Sunday morning Lancelots
Gladly take the short straw
And their best friend to the store
Right out of bed
For the ones they love.
Wandering the isles
Like lost crusaders on a quest
For their Queen's desires,
Looking like the morning after
The night before.
For coffee and milk, tampons and bread
When they'd rather be
Back home instead.
Snuggled up next to Guinevere
All warm in her bed.
Who said Sunday morning chivalry is dead?
Their bed head hair
Sticking out like antennas
On a microwave tower,
They're off to the store
Under loves power, for caffeine...
I always wear a hat.
Wandering the store
Yammering in silence to themselves
At that ungodly hour... for love.
I never noticed it until today
Six of us shopping all in the same way,
We even had on some of the same things

When we went up to pay.
Ancient knights at the beginning of their day
On a quest for coffee creamer.
While their best friend waits patiently in the car
No questions asked, nothing wrong.
They wouldn't have it any other way.
They're just happy to go along.

Clothesline Sheets

The hot summer breeze
Smelled of black berries and licorice.
Cedar and oak with a hint of basil.
That's where the clothesline was,
Near the garden.
One more reason I love the summer.
It has its own scent, its own flavor,
An aroma that blooms in the heat of the day
And rides on the wind.
Leaving the memory of it's breath
In your fresh cleans sheets like a lipstick kiss
Left by a lover on the bathroom mirror
Under the steam.
Something to take to bed with you
In the moment, from the day
When the wind blows the flavors of the month
Into your dreams under the covers.
Clothesline sheets are dream catchers
For your nose, your skin, your hair.
A compass pointing you toward a day, a year,
A season when life was slower,
Easier and more patient.
Patient enough to hang
Freshly laundered sheets
On a wire, a rope, in the sun
On a summer day in the breeze until they're dry.
Smooth and seasoned with lavender, jasmine, and wild plum.

Billowing genoas snapping
Gently upwards against
A cloudless blue summer sky
From the clothesline they're tied to.
This is where the sheets, towels, and unders
That were hung to dry in the summer breeze
Are baked, and scented,
Sealing in the aroma of the day
By the afternoon sun.
When the moon came up
It shone like diamonds on your skin
In the sweat glistening on your breasts
As they moisten your fresh clothesline sheets from the day
In the heat of a summer night.
The scent of lavender and raspberries
Flavor your skin,
While a hint of blackberries and cedar on him
Drifts across the room...
The aroma from Mother's perfume is
So sweet it is almost visible in the moonlight.
Being warmed and awakened
By the love of two who became one.
Fresh and delicious under the moonlight where lovers meet...
And lie in each others arms when they're done,
Under the fragrant crispness
Of a clothesline sheet.

A Last Taste Of Summer

Nothing signals the end of summer
Like the blackberry stains
On your fingers
At the end of August and early September
When it's still getting over eighty degrees,
And the smell of blackberries as they linger
At the end of summer is what I remember
As one of my favorite memories.
Blackberries waiting plump and full on the vine...
To be found by wild lips and eager fingers,
When the beginning of Autumn
Is pouring color into the leaves
Then spilling them onto the ground.
The long walks in the fall
With your sweatshirt tied around
Your waist or up over your shoulders
As the evenings are growing darker sooner
And the mornings are starting
Out a little colder.
The afternoon walks down along the river
Through the fields and into the woods
Are lined with that juicy black purple delight
And the flavor it delivers
When you pop them into your mouth
Exploding with sweet summers ink in every bite.
A tasty reminder that fall is coming.
As you look to the skies
And hear the geese calling

From their formations
Heading south in their flight.
And know there's joy in berry picking
And lots of purple finger licking
The end of summer
From your finger tips, right?

Early In The Morning Or Late At Night

Every night when he comes home
His circumstances are always the same.
First he unlocks the door with his keys
Then he greets his cat when she calls his name;
She's always the first one he sees.
He puts down his pack,
Hang's his coat with his hat
On their hook beside the door.
It's déjà vu all over again
Just like the night before.

All is quiet everyone is in bed
As he bends to turn on his Mac.
He pours a glass of his favorite red
And wonders before he hits the sac...
Somewhere this is early in the morning
For others it's late at night.
It doesn't really matter to him
In the glow of the computer light.
This is the time he cherishes,
When he finally gets to sit down and write.
From this space somewhere in between
Come tales of the heart
From beginning to the end
Where he's more than a witness
If you know what I mean,
From places we've all been too, over and again.

He brings them up and writes them down
On pieces of paper with his favorite pen,
Until he's too tired to see to write,
Which is probably just as well in the end.
When it's early in the morning or late at night.
And his glass is as empty
As his heart has been before.
Until tomorrow when he comes home again
And pours his heart out through his pen,
When he sits down in the quiet
To write once more.

Phil Pochurek

Bella's BIG Adventure

The universe works in strange ways. This is a story about a little black kitten named Bella and how her universe changed for six days in July.

In Bella's world, everything was BIG. Including her family, which is how Bella came to live with her family in the beginning.

It all started when the mom of the house had to stop at the store on her way home from work to get some cream cheese for the icing of a birthday cake she was baking for a friend. As the mom approached the entrance of the store, a young girl was holding a black kitten in a cardboard box with a sign on it that said "FREE." The mom asked the girl if the kitten had a name. The girl smiled and said her name was "Bella" and that "it meant *beautiful* in Italian."

Bella was the last of a litter of eight kitties and barely eight weeks old—just a little bigger than a tennis ball. The mom went into the store. Her heart was taken by the kitten outside, but she knew better than to make such a big decision without asking her family first, and most of all asking the family cat "Mr. Kitty" if he minded having a little sister. Then she thought about her black cat, Ninja, who had died two years before after seventeen long, loving years with her. Ninja wasn't any bigger than Bella when she found him, and that did it. The mom of the house had made up her mind. If Bella was still out in front of the store when the mom left, she would take her home. The mom dashed down the aisles, found the cream cheese she needed for the cake, and made her way to the front of the store. She looked out the store windows for the girl holding Bella but couldn't see her anywhere. Her heart sank as she took her grocery sack and headed out the door to her car. There on the curb sat the girl with Bella in her arms, and that's how Bella's life with her new family began. From a cardboard box to a new family, food, a bed, and a big brother, Mr. Kitty.

Before the mom came home that evening, she called ahead and said she had a big surprise for everyone. Soon she was home. She walked into the kitchen and sat her grocery sack down, her arms wrapped around a cardboard box. She sat it down, and they all anxiously looked inside. It was the smallest big surprise they had ever seen. There was Bella staring up at them, scared but excited to be home. She was cute as a bug and small enough to fit in a teacup.

Well, things were certainly going to be different around their house. It had been a long time since they had had a baby in the house—about four years since Mr. Kitty had come home in a similar way with the dad one day. Now, all this excitement on the countertop of course had drawn Mr. Kitty's attention. This was the first time Bella would meet her BIG brother.

I'm not sure what Mr. Kitty was thinking, except maybe "Is it staying?" But his surprise was certainly not as big as Bella's. Every hair on her little body stood straight out like she was electrified. She became twice her size and was off in a shot.

It's amazing how fast something so small can move when it's scared. As for Mr. Kitty, he acted indifferent, but they really thought his feelings were hurt. He couldn't understand why they would need another cat that he would have to share his family with, and eventually babysit.

Then, as he turned to leave, the funniest thing happened. Out of nowhere Bella came running back and, in one flying pounce, jumped on Mister's back in full kitty playing mode. Mister went down like a rock but quickly rolled over and had Bella pinned in an understanding way that conveyed, play or not, he was the first and biggest cat of the house.

But as soon as he let Bella up, she was back at him again. Bella had a big brother and loved him from the first day they met. Mr. Kitty would take a little longer to make up his mind.

Slowly, things began to change around the house. There was a baby in the house now, and she demanded attention. She had a litter box that needed cleaning, and she ate all the time, so her food and water had to be checked twice as often as Mr. Kitty's. After all, she was a growing kitten.

Days turned into weeks as the summer rolled on, and soon it was the Fourth of July. Bella got to see her first sparkler.

By mid-July, Bella had grown quite noticeably into a wonderful little kitten. And Mr. Kitty had finally given in to the fact that she was here to stay. Their wrestling matches were a daily routine now and a regular circus to watch. Mr. Kitty would sit like the sphinx while Bella would climb all over him, chewing his ears and chasing his tail. This usually lasted for half an hour or so until Mr. Kitty had had enough and would ask to be let out. They would keep Bella inside to give Mister a break, and she would promptly go off and take a nap. Growing kittens, just like children, need their rest too! It's hard work getting big.

Bella loved to play hide-and-seek. Any place she could find to be out of sight, she thought was great. Of course, being a baby, Bella thought if she couldn't see you then you couldn't see her. This was a fun game for everyone. If Bella could get inside, underneath, behind, or on top of something, she would. She would get inside a paper bag, behind a door, or under a towel. Bella loved to hide. Sometimes you had to look hard because she was so good at being quiet. Bella's family loved this game, but one day soon, Bella would learn an important lesson about hiding.

It was a Tuesday in a week when the mom and the daughter of the house were gone on a vacation together and wouldn't be home until Saturday. That left the dad home alone with Bella and Mr. Kitty.

The girls had been gone since Saturday, and everything had been fine until Tuesday. That's when Bella's universe changed.

The dad had just finished doing his morning chores: watering the garden and flowers, sweeping the garage, and washing the cars. He was glad to get these things done early because it had been so hot the last few days. He also was playing hide-and-seek with Bella and paying extra attention to her because there were a lot more trucks and traffic in the neighborhood than usual. The house right next door on the corner was beginning to be built, and two houses across the street were also being worked on. Bella knew some of the workers because she liked to hide in the grass and watch them hammer and saw boards for the house. This had never been a problem before, but today was going to be a little different.

Now that Bella was getting older and bigger, she had gradually been given a little more freedom. Lately, when Bella's family went somewhere for short periods of time, instead of shutting her in the laundry room with her food, water, and litter box, Bella had been able to stay in the garage. And because it had been so hot, the dad had been leaving the side door out to the backyard open. That way Bella could come and go when she wanted to and get to her food and water that were in the garage. She could also play with Mr. Kitty in the yard, chasing grasshoppers when they landed on the lawn.

Today was special for the dad because he was going to have lunch with some friends to celebrate a birthday. The dad was a little concerned about all the extra workers around but decided Bella would be OK—that he wouldn't stay long at the birthday party.

So a little before eleven, the dad loved Bella up and warned her about all the traffic and to be careful—that she should stay in her yard, and he would be home soon. As the garage door closed, and the dad drove off to lunch, Bella's adventure was about to begin.

What the dad didn't know was how easy and how often Bella would scoot under the fence in the backyard and be outside, free in the world.

Bella was so excited! She had never seen so many trucks around her corner before. Especially with their doors and tailgates wide open.

There were plumbers, electricians, landscapers, carpenters, and painters everywhere. Bella was so excited she didn't know where to begin.

There were so many different sights and sounds, even smells coming out of all the trucks, that she just watched all the workers for a while at first. Everyone was so busy, and Bella so small, they didn't even notice her as she worked her way around the construction sites.

Bella had so much fun running and hiding from everyone that she didn't even notice it when, after she had jumped inside a big cardboard box to hide, one of the workers added some more scrap paper to it and carried it out to his truck, to go back to his shop. This was when Bella's big adventure was about to begin. Little did Bella know she was about to have a lunch date of her own that would last six long days and nights. The dad came home from his lunch date around twelve thirty, just like he had planned, because he didn't want Bella to be alone when things were so busy around the house next door. He was glad to see there weren't so many trucks in the street when he returned. Some had left for the day, and others had gone for lunch. When the dad pulled into the driveway, he hit the garage door opener button and waited for Bella to come running out. He thought it was a little odd when she didn't and decided he had better look for her when he got out. He walked all around the house, searching the front and back yards in all of Bella's favorite hiding places, but there was no sign of her anywhere. Now he was starting to worry. He called her name some more, "Bella," Bella," then louder "Bella, Bella, BELLA."

But no baby kitty, and the dad's heart began to sink, but he did find Mr. Kitty, which made him feel even worse because Bella loved Mister and was never very far from him whenever he was around.

So the dad began talking to all of the construction workers to see if they had noticed a little black kitty playing around where they were working. But the answer was always the same, NO. The Dad was heartbroken. He walked and walked and called. He asked all the neighbors that lived close and rode his bicycle around the areas that were farther away from home, asking strangers if they had seen Bella and calling her name, "Bella, Bella."

He even had a picture to show people, but no one had seen Bella. They were very nice and said they would call if they did. He had put off admitting she was lost because he didn't want to believe it was true, but he realized now he had to do it. The dad made up posters with Bella's picture and phone number on it that said:

LITTLE BLACK BELLA CAT
IS LOST—PLEASE CALL: 614-7271

He put them all around the neighborhood, and then put an ad in the newspaper. It read like the posters, only it had where, when, and about what time she was lost. He should have known better than to leave her on her own when things were so busy around the house that day, and he should have put her name tags and collar on her like he was supposed to when the girls left on their vacation, instead of putting it off. That was another hurt he wasn't looking forward to: telling the girls.

He hadn't heard from them for a couple of days, which was good. That meant that they were having so much fun in San Francisco that they were too busy and tired to call home just yet. This would give him a little more time to find Bella before they asked about her, if they did.

The dad wasn't quite sure what to do, but he eventually decided that he would wait to tell them about Bella until after they were home. He couldn't see any sense in ruining their vacation with such bad news. He could only hope to find Bella before Saturday when he had to pick up the girls at the airport, and eventually tell them Bella was lost.

By Wednesday, the dad had searched everywhere around the area near their house, and still no sign of Bella. Behind their house was a busy road with houses on one side and wide open fields and countryside on the other. At first he thought Bella may have followed Mr. Kitty on one of his walkabouts and gotten lost. But if Bella had gone with Mr. Kitty, she would have stayed right with him because she loved him so much.

The dad could only hope that's what happened, and that after one of his country walks, Mr. Kitty would bring Bella home.

The worst part about Bella being gone was not knowing what happened to her. He thought about this as he walked the long road beside the ditches, looking to see if maybe a car had hit Bella. He tried to put this out of his mind as he searched and called for her, but if he found her at least he would know that's what had happened, and he would bring her home. After he had searched the roadside thoroughly, he was satisfied that being hit by a car wasn't what had happened to Bella. He gave an exhausted sigh of relief and gained a spark of hope, which showed in his step. When he returned home, he called animal shelters and reported her missing. He also called all the veterinarians in his area and emergency animal hospitals in case someone had brought Bella in. Then, of course, his last call was the newspaper.

The woman in the advertising department of the newspaper helped the dad write his ad for Bella and was very positive and reassuring; she said that they had a very high success rate for finding people's pets. This made the dad feel good and gave him a glimmer of hope, knowing that soon the whole town would know that Bella was missing. Then, hopefully, whoever had Bella would return her to her family.

It was Friday night when the phone rang and two happy voices from San Francisco were on the line waiting to talk to the dad. It was late, and his girls were tired and excited from their day in the big city, so their conversation was short.

The dad was thankful for that and that he didn't have to answer any questions about the kitties. He would see the girls soon enough at the airport on Saturday, and he wanted every minute of their vacation together to be as happy as it could be. He hated to have to be the spoiler with such bad news and wanted to wait as long as he could to tell them.

Meanwhile, somewhere across town, someone was scared and lost. It turns out that the box Bella was in was picked up by a building contractor, thrown into the back of his van, and driven across town to the main office. Behind that office was a fenced-in parking lot for all of the work vans at the end of the day, and that is where Bella ended up.

Bella was so scared she didn't even come out of her box until after dark—only to find that she'd been locked in a van with no food or water and no way to get out. She began to cry.

Poor Bella. She had no idea where she was, or where her family was and why they didn't come and get her. She was scared, thirsty, and hungry and had nowhere to go potty. Bella had to decide what to do. She was getting tired from crying, and mad too that no one heard her and came to get her out! The parking lot she was in was surrounded by fences to people's backyards. Some of the yards even had dogs that heard her cries and barked and growled back, which scared Bella even more. A busy highway nearby made a lot of car noise, so no one was able to hear Bella's cries except the dogs.

Bella finally quit crying after about twenty minutes and just looked out the window at the parking lot. She started to make her plan.

Bella knew she was pretty much stuck where she was for the night, so she tried to make the best of it. At least she was safe from the animals of the night. She crawled all over the van, looking under all the seats and behind everything to see if there might be something to eat. She could smell something, but she couldn't find it. Finally, she ended up back in the box she came in. Inside her box was an empty takeout sack from a hamburger restaurant, where she found them: six long French fries must have spilled out when the contractor was having his lunch, and the last bite of a bacon cheeseburger. Wow, Bella was so excited she started purring and eating at the same time.

After Bella's wonderful stowaway dinner of leftovers, she was tired. After all, she had had a busy day. But now that she had some food in her tummy, she felt a lot better and wasn't quite so scared of what had happened to her.

She curled up on top of a box in the back of the van just below the window so no one could see her, but she could rise up and look out if she heard something.

Bella was sound asleep when she heard it the first time. She thought she was dreaming and closed her eyes, and then she heard it again. This time she woke all the way up and was on alert. She heard what sounded like little claws climbing and scratching on the back of the van. Then she heard the strangest noise. It was kind of a chortle, purring, clicking noise, when all of a sudden the door handle to the back of the van started to wiggle. Bella was scared now. Someone was trying to get in, and it wasn't a human. What was it?

Bella was so scared, but she had to know. She slowly rose up to look out her window, and there staring back at her was the biggest cat she had ever seen, and it was wearing a mask. It was trying to break into the van. Bella didn't know what to do. Then she remembered, from when she had driven with her family, what they had done before they started to drive. They always pushed down the little button by the window after they put their seatbelts on. It was the only thing Bella could think of to do.

Quickly, she reached over with her little paw and pushed down on the button. It worked! The door locked, and Bella was safe. The raccoon tried several more times to open the door, then decided to crawl down and look for food somewhere else. Bella was so relieved, except for one thing. She'd never know if that big scary raccoon was after the hamburger she ate for dinner or was going to eat her! She was so glad she never had to find out.

The next time Bella heard something outside, it was the gate to the parking lot being unlocked and opened so the workmen could get to their vans and head out to their jobs. Bella had to be ready if her plan was going to work.

Slowly, she peeked out of her window to see who was there. The first man was getting into his truck and leaving. That's when Bella heard it. Someone at the front of her van was opening the door. At the same time, Bella heard footsteps coming around to the back of the van where she was sitting crouched on top of her box, waiting for the door to open. Bella knew she would have to act fast if she were going to get out of the van and on her way back home.

Bella was ready. She heard the footsteps right behind the van where she was sitting. She could hear the man set down his tool box and the sound of his keys as he got them out of his pocket and put them in the lock on the back door. He never suspected the surprise he was about to receive when he opened the door. Bella watched the handle turn, and then the door swung open wide; it was now or never. After the man opened the door, he turned to pick up his toolbox, and that was all that Bella needed. In one big leap, she bounded out of the van onto the back of the workman who was bent over and then out into the parking lot and under a pile of lumber like a bolt of lightning. The workman had no idea what had just happened. He jumped up with a whoop and a holler and looked all around to see if anyone or anything was near, but Bella was already out of the van and well-hidden where she could watch the men leave before she came out of her hiding spot.

It was Wednesday now, and Bella had been away from her home and family for a whole day and night. She was scared, lonesome, and hungry and didn't know quite what to do. Bella needed a plan, but she didn't have her big brother, Mr. Kitty, around to help her and most of all protect her from other animals and keep her safe. She was all alone, but this time she didn't cry. She knew feeling sorry for herself wasn't going to get her back home. As soon as Bella felt safe enough to come out of her hiding place, she looked around at what would be her new home for the next few days. Slowly she worked her way around all the fences that surrounded the parking lot. Surely she could find someone who could help her get back home.

The first fence she came to had a nice yard, with lots of grass and flowers and even a garden. Bella liked this yard and was just about to go under the fence when she saw him. Running toward her at full speed, barking all the way, was the family dog, and he was BIG! Just like the one that lived next door to her at her own house. Bella was petrified. She didn't move and could only hope that the fence would hold "Jasper." She heard a family yelling his name from inside the house when he came charging up to the fence.

Bella was so scared that all her hair stood on end, and she puffed up to twice her size, hissing and spitting. These were the only two things she knew how to do that Mr. Kitty had taught her for when she was in trouble. Of course, this only made her as big as a softball instead of a tennis ball, but the fence held back Jasper. Bella moved along to the next yard, with Jasper wailing and barking at her all the way. Eventually, Jasper went back to his porch, and things were quiet again.

Bella was thankful for that as she climbed up on to a pile of boards so she could look into the next yard to see if anyone was home.

Bella sat on a pile of wood high off the ground where she could watch everything. Being up high made Bella feel safe. In fact, Bella felt so safe and comfortable sitting on her woodpile under the shade of a big oak tree that she fell asleep. It's a good thing that Bella picked the summer for her big adventure because it stayed warm outside even at night.

When Bella woke up, it was dark and the streetlights were on. She looked over to the house she was watching, and there was still no sign of anyone, especially a dog. So Bella decided to go exploring. She walked along the top of the fence until she came to the oak tree and jumped across to its trunk where she climbed down into the yard. Carefully, Bella looked all around for any signs of other animals. When she felt safe, she snuck up to the house and looked in the glass patio door, but no one was home. They were probably out on an adventure of their own—only they knew how to get back home when they were done.

This made Bella homesick and sad, but at least she had a safe place to spend the night. Bella climbed up onto the barbecue and slept on top of the vinyl cover. She went to bed hungry for the first time she could remember, which really made her appreciate and miss her family for taking such good care of her and loving her so much.

She knew if she ever got back home, she would never run off again.

Thursday morning came early and warm. Bella woke up with the slam of a car door from the parking lot where she spent her first night.

Bella looked around to see if anything had changed in her yard during the night, but she was right: no one was home. Bella thought this was okay after all and decided she would stay here until the owners came home. At least she would have a place to come back to when she went out to look for food.

Bella jumped down from her barbecue perch onto the patio and began to walk all around her new yard. She tried to avoid the side of the fence that Jasper was on. No sense in getting him all worked up and making a lot of noise. This is how Jasper would help Bella find her breakfast. In the far corner of the yard, not far from the oak tree that Bella had climbed down from, there was a post in the ground. All around the base of it were breadcrumbs and sunflower seeds. Bella was used to eating dried food at home or "crunchies" but had never tried bread or seeds. Bella was so happy to find something to eat on her own that she gladly crunched down the spilled crumbs that were on the ground. Bella was making quite a little racket of her own while she was eating when she heard it the first time.

In mid-bite, Bella quit chewing and went on alert! She listened and looked around to see where the noise was coming from. Suddenly, a chunk of bread hit her right on the head. Bella jumped back, then looked up to see if she could see who had hit her. Up on the platform above her she heard it again and noticed sunflower seed shells occasionally raining down from above to where she was below. Bella watched and waited to see who was making all this noise and spilling her breakfast over the side for her to eat.

Then, just as Bella was about to start eating again, there it was, with a little face with pointy ears and a big bushy tail, looking down over the side of the tray that was nailed on top of the post.

Bella had just met her first squirrel. Bella froze on the spot. She wasn't quite sure what to do. Mr. Kitty had only told her one story about squirrels, and only enough for her to know that this was one.

The squirrel continued to eat while he watched Bella from up on top of his feeder. He didn't seem to be too threatened or bothered by Bella as he had his breakfast. He did knock some more bread crumbs over the side for Bella to eat though. Whether the squirrel knocked them by accident or on purpose, Bella was thankful. Then just as quickly as he had come, the squirrel jumped off his feeder over to the fence and back up the oak tree where he lived. Bella couldn't believe how fast and far the squirrel could run and jump. It was just like the story Mr. Kitty had told her one day while they were resting under a tree in her family's backyard. This made Bella homesick again but more determined to find her way back home to her own yard and family and, of course, Mr. Kitty.

Bella spent the rest of the day exploring her new backyard, learning every corner, every nook and cranny, in case she had to hide or escape from danger. She also hoped whoever lived in the house might come home, be friendly, and find her—maybe even help her to get back home.

Before Bella knew it, it was early evening and the sun was setting on another day. Bella felt safe in her new yard and thought she might stay here one more night before she explored the last yard that bordered the parking lot she arrived in.

Once again darkness fell, the streetlights came on, and the stars came out. It was another beautiful summer night. Bella wished that Mr. Kitty were here to share the night with her and hear her story about meeting her first squirrel, but that would have to wait. It was bedtime, and Bella had found a new place to sleep for the night.

On the side of the yard next to the fence was a woodpile with a tarp over it. The wood was stacked up as high as the fence, so Bella was able to see all around her much better. This made her feel a lot safer. Most of all, Bella was able to look down into the yard next door. That was the only yard she hadn't explored yet. From what she could see by the moonlight, it was smaller than the yard she was in and a little more cluttered. She could hardly wait to go exploring in it. She decided to wait until tomorrow when she could see in the daylight if it was a friendly yard or not. She didn't like surprises, especially dangerous ones. She felt in the daylight she had a better chance of getting away if something or someone were after her. Soon after Bella had reached her roost on top of the woodpile, she was fast asleep under a warm July moon.

Friday morning came early from on top of the woodpile. Bella watched the squirrel climb down out of his oak tree to have breakfast on his feeder. She could also see Jasper being let outside for his first morning run in his yard. The workmen were beginning to arrive in the parking lot behind the back fence to load their trucks with their tools. Bella liked it up on the woodpile; she could see all around her in every direction and felt safe because of it.

But now she was watching the house next door—the only one whose yard she hadn't been in yet. It was small but nice. It had a little patio with a cover, several tables and chairs, and, of course, a barbecue.

Brightly colored flowers grew all around the yard just inside the fence. This looked like the perfect place for Bella to try to meet someone and tell them her story. The most important thing Bella did notice and was thankful for was that there weren't any dogs! That would make things a lot easier, and from what Bella could tell, there were not kitties either. Bella thought these people must be lonely, so she decided to make it her job to cheer them up and give them some of her best purring love.

Bella watched who she thought must be the mom through the windows of the house most of the morning in the kitchen and laundry room. This mom was probably doing her family chores for the day much like Bella's family did. Bella was so excited to meet the people who lived in this house, but by mid-morning the sun was up and it was too hot to stay on the woodpile any longer. So Bella climbed down, had a drink of water out of the squirrel's water bowl by his feeder and a few breadcrumbs off the ground, and then strolled over to take an afternoon nap under a nice, cool hydrangea bush. Bella knew she had better get rested up if she was going to meet this new family.

Bella woke up around six thirty that evening to the sounds of laughter and music; voices were coming from over the fence by the woodpile. And a deliciously familiar smell of barbecued chicken was drifting in the air like a smoke cloud of dinner. The scent was so yummy you could taste it.

Bella came out from under her bush and ran across the yard to the woodpile. She made it to the top in two jumps. Bella was so excited. This was better than she had ever hoped. There on the other side of the fence, the yard was full of people. The barbecue was going, tiki torches were lit, and music was playing. It was a summer party—just what Bella needed to meet as many people as she could. Hopefully, someone might be able to help her get back home. Someone had to know she was missing. Bella walked across the woodpile along the fence until she was right above the people closest to the fence. She sat down, and in her sweetest Bella voice, said hello.

No one heard her tiny voice at first because the music was a little loud. When there was a break in the music, Bella tried again, "Mew." Her little voice was more of a squeak. She hadn't even grown into a full meow yet.

The lady next to Bella looked up and smiled at her in such a warm and friendly way that Bella offered no resistance when the woman reached for her. The lady held her close to her heart; Bella could feel it beating, and she began to purr. The lady smelled good too! She reminded her of the girls in her family at her home and wondered if they knew she was missing yet. This was the first time since Bella had been gone that she had let someone touch her.

The lady cooed and stroked Bella and kissed and hugged her. Then she began to take her all around the party and ask everyone if she was their kitty. This is exactly what Bella wanted.

Bella spent the rest of the party being passed around and held by everyone there until the only ones who were left were the family that lived there and that first lady who had picked Bella up earlier in the evening. She was a neighbor several houses down the street and had stayed to help clean up after the party.

The woman held and carried Bella everywhere, like she was a china doll, constantly loving her and petting her. Bella couldn't get enough. After the last few days she had had, this was like heaven to her.

By the time everything was cleaned up, the women had saved quite a pile of chicken for Bella. They cut it into small pieces and put it on a plate for her right beside a big bowl of fresh, cold, clean water. Bella had forgotten how thirsty she was until she started to drink. When Bella was done, the mom of the house picked her up and carried her inside to their back porch, where they had made a nice, soft bed for her right beside another bowl of fresh water and a small plate of chicken. Bella couldn't believe how things had changed.

She went from breadcrumbs to barbecued chicken, and from the woodpile outside to a soft warm bed inside, safe and sound.

And that's how Bella spent Friday night, her fourth night away from home and on her own. She watched as the lady who had found her earlier that evening was leaving. The woman turned to give Bella one more pat on the head and said, "If no one comes to claim her and you can't find her a home, I'll take her."

Bella knew now who would be her new owner if she couldn't find her way back to her own family.

By midnight, everyone was gone. The little house seemed to be bigger without so many people in it.

Bella was so tired from all the excitement that she was ready for bed. When the lady put Bella down in the laundry room on top of her own special blanket, her eyes closed as soon as her head touched her bed. Tonight, she would sleep well and rest up for tomorrow. Bella had some ideas of her own about how Saturday would unfold and couldn't wait to close her eyes so she could wake up.

She was ready to tell EVERYONE about what had happened to her. The only thing wrong with that was no matter what Bella said, it all came out the same: *mew, mew, mew, mew, mew, MEW,...mew.*

Back across town, just the opposite was happening. A dad, unable to close his eyes and get any sleep, lay waiting for an alarm to go off in the morning. He would need sleep and energy when the time came to pass on the bad news, to tell his girls that he had lost their kitten. If only he had gotten Bella's nametag and collar when he was supposed to, all of this might have been avoided. If only he had locked Bella in the garage while it was so busy around the house that afternoon. If, If, If! For such a little word, it carried such big consequences. He reached for the alarm just before it went off at six thirty. He might as well get up because he was already awake. It was another beautiful summer day. He had chatted with the girls briefly last night about picking them up at the airport today but mostly listened to them talk about their last night on the town in San Francisco—and still without any mention of the cats. At least up until now their vacation was perfect. They would fly home happy and tired, and he would have a little more time to think about how he would tell them about Bella.

By eleven o'clock, he had long been shaved and showered and had drank too much coffee. He would be taking his daughter's girlfriend with him to the airport. He didn't know how bringing her would affect the bad news he had to tell the girls, but he hoped it would help having her there. She already knew the whole story and felt bad about the situation, but reminded the dad not to give up; there was always a chance of finding Bella. This made the dad feel better as he turned the car onto the freeway and drove toward the airport.

The drive would take about an hour and a half. About ten minutes after they left the house, his daughter's friend fell asleep. This gave the dad a few final minutes to decide how to tell his girls about Bella. Usually, the drive to the airport seemed to take longer than it should, either from traffic or weather, but today neither of those factors were an issue. Traffic was light, and the weather was beautiful. They seemed to be making record time. The dad tried to relax and think clearly about what he was going to say, but bad news is bad news, and he knew there would be tears. That was the last thing he wanted to see on the girls' faces. He hated to be the one to take their smiles away after the great week they had just spent together.

They arrived at the airport with plenty of time to spare and found that the plane was right on schedule. Soon, the dad's secret would be out, and he would have to go through the pain he had suffered all week long looking for Bella all over again, only worse. Now his girls would be sad too.

The dad and his daughter's friend waited at one end of the airport concourse while the girls arrived at the other. He called them on his cell phone to find out where they were, and they all agreed to meet at the baggage claim area. Hugs and kisses and smiles were nonstop for about ten minutes; then they began their walk out to the car.

The girls were so excited about their trip but glad to be traveling home. They could sleep in their own beds tonight. After the car was loaded, they headed out of the parkade and off toward the freeway. Talking nonstop, they took turns telling stories and finishing each other's sentences. They were so happy and excited to be going home. After about forty-five minutes, they had finally run out of stories to tell and were ready to ask the dad how his week had been. The young girls were chatting in the back seat when the mom leaned over from the passenger seat and gave the dad a kiss. She said she had missed him and missed her kitties too. How were they? This was it—the moment the dad had dreaded, the sad truth. He said he missed them, too, especially Bella—that she was missing. Suddenly, the car became quiet. Nobody said anything until the mom finally spoke up with tears in her eyes; she asked what happened.

The dad told his story about the birthday lunch and coming home to find Bella missing. He told them about the long days and nights of searching for Bella, calling her name and talking to all of their neighbors. That after Tuesday the dad's vacation was pretty much spent looking for Bella.

The daughter in the back seat understood that sometimes these things happen and gave her dad a hug and told him she was sorry he had such an awful time while they were gone. She would help him look for Bella when they got home, and with all of them looking, they were sure to find her. The front seat beside the dad was a lot quieter. The mom really loved Bella. She reminded her of her kitty that passed away last summer because he was so old. She found him in much the same way she came to find Bella. She was in the right place at the right time. She really thought she had another chance to have her old kitty back again through Bella.

As soon as they got home, the dad began unloading the car, and the mom started walking the neighborhood, calling for Bella. She hoped that if Bella could just hear her voice, Bella would come running back.

Dinner was quiet that evening. Mr. Kitty was around to welcome the girls back and was extra affectionate to try to cheer the girls up and ease the hurt of Bella being gone. He was probably the only one who really knew what happened to Bella that day, and he couldn't tell them either.

It was great having the girls home, and the dad finally got his first night of good sleep since Tuesday. Sunday morning, the dad got up and made French toast for the girls and brought the mom a cup of coffee and the paper. He showed her the ad he had placed for Bella in the lost pet column. This was their last big hope of finding her. People from all over town and in the county read the paper. Surely someone who had seen Bella or found her would read the paper and see her ad.

LITTLE BLACK BELLA CAT
IS LOST—PLEASE CALL: 614-7271

It was a long shot, but it made the mom feel better to see the ad in the paper with all the other lost animals, most of them with FOUND stamped across them.

This was just the hope she needed to cheer her up. Sunday was her last day off before she had to go back to work with her bad news. What she didn't know is that everyone already new about Bella at her work and was ready to cheer her up when she got back. The dad had to work on Monday too but not until the afternoon. He decided he would ride his bicycle in a different area and look for Bella before he went to work.

Sunday night at dinner, Bella's family included her in their grace and sent prayers and wishes out to her to keep her safe and help her to find her way back home.

The universe works in strange and wonderful ways. Across town, Bella's family's wishes were being answered. Bella had just finished her second dish of steak with a side saucer of half-and-half cream. She was so full and content she fell asleep on the lap of the lady who had found her on Friday night at the barbecue. The woman reminded the friend who Bella was staying with that if no one claimed her by Tuesday, she would gladly take her, especially because the friend's rental agreement said "no pets."

Bella liked both ladies. They were very kind to her and always had something for her to eat. Bella knew that if her family didn't come for her pretty soon, she might never see them again.

    She went to bed Sunday night with a full tummy and hopes that her family hadn't given up on her yet. If only they could know that she was safe and all right.

    Vacations were over back at Bella's family's house. The mom got up early Monday morning and went for a walk in the neighborhood before work with the hope of finding Bella before she went to work for the day. But with no sign of Bella, the mom came home, took her shower, got dressed, and left for work just as the sun was coming up. An hour went by, and then the dad got up and had his first cup of coffee with Mr. Kitty. Things were beginning to get back to normal, except for one thing: their baby was still missing. The daughter was still sound asleep and would be for several more hours. This is when the dad usually went for his bike ride. A quick twenty miles every morning before work always helped him jump-start his day.

    When the dad returned from his ride, his daughter was still sleeping, just as he left her. It was about ten thirty now, and he was ready for his second cup of coffee, when he noticed the message light on the answering machine was on, showing one call. He poured his coffee and pushed the button. It's probably a good thing he wasn't holding his cup, or he would have dropped it. The woman on the message was answering the ad in the paper about Bella. He couldn't believe his ears. He scribbled down her number and called her back as fast as he could. She was so nice and described Bella perfectly. She said she wasn't sure if it was Bella because they lived clear across town. Then she asked the dad if there was any construction going on near his house. She said her backyard fence was against a construction company's parking lot. Bella had come over the fence Friday night during a barbecue, and the woman had had her since then. The dad told her they were building a house right next door to theirs and two across the street. Then he said he would be right over. He didn't know how it happened, but he thought this had to be Bella. He could hardly drive, he was so excited. He told his daughter he had to run an errand, and he would be right back. He asked her if there was anything he could get her while he was out. She smiled. "You could bring Bella home, Dad." "I'll see what I can do," he said as he practically ran to the car. All the way across town, he kept hoping it was Bella. Everything fit into place. He thought all along something like this might have happened to her.

He knocked on the door, and a lady answered. She was so nice, and when she opened the door, there was Bella! Sweet as ever.

She didn't seem as small anymore as she was before she left. She must have grown a little through this whole ordeal, on the outside as well as on the inside. The lady picked her up and handed her to the dad. Bella was already purring when he took ahold of her. This was Bella all right. The dad tried to pay the lady for her trouble, but she wouldn't hear of it. She said Bella was a pure joy. She would have liked to have kept Bella for herself, but her lease didn't allow her to have pets. She was ready that afternoon to give Bella to her girlfriend who had fallen in love with the kitty since she first found her.

Bella's caretaker thought she would look one more place before she handed the kitten over to her friend, and that's when she saw the dad's ad in the Sunday paper.

She didn't think it could possibly be Bella but thought she had better try calling anyway just in case. Her hunch paid off. She was glad Bella was going back to her own home, and so was the dad. This was everything he had hoped would happen.

He thanked the lady again and took Bella out to the car. She was a little afraid, having the run of the car while the car was moving, but soon Bella settled down in the dad's lap and purred all the way home.

When they got back home, Mr. Kitty was waiting by the back door like a one-kitty welcome home party. The two cats sniffed noses and rubbed tails just like old buds. Mr. Kitty was the true test in identifying Bella. The dad held his breath for a moment until Bella and Mr. Kitty began to play with each other again, just as if nothing had ever happened.

The dad picked up Bella and took her inside. His daughter was watching TV on the couch when Bella came into the room. Bella snuck around to the end of the couch and peeked over the arm to surprise her friend.

The daughter let out a hoop and a scream that even scared Bella. Tears and laughter came next, with lots of hugs. It was time now for the dad to go to work. He told his daughter not to call the mom, that she should keep Bella in her room and think of her own way to surprise the mom after she came home.

Before the dad went to work, he went to the pet store and had a tag made with Bella's name, address, and phone number on it, and bought her a pretty pink collar with a little tiny bell on it. He put the tags on her collar, and then put the collar on Bella. He knew it wouldn't keep her from getting lost again, but at least this time whoever found her would know who she was and where she lived.

Then the dad was off to work. He hugged his girl and Bella and was out the door—happy now that their family was all together again.

His daughter was happy, too, and so was Bella, who was so thankful to be home. Bella had gotten to say hello to everyone in her family except the mom. She could hardly wait for her to come home. She spent the rest of the afternoon with the daughter and Mr. Kitty. This had been quite an exciting day, and by late afternoon, Bella was pretty tired. She found her way down the hall to the daughter's room and hopped up on her bed and curled up for a little nap. She wanted to be rested when the mom came home so she had lots of energy for purring while she was getting hugged.

The daughter closed her door to hide her surprise for her mom. At around four thirty, the daughter heard the garage door go up and the mom's car pull in after a long, sad first day back at work. She knew the mom would be tired from not getting much sleep while worrying about Bella.

When the mom walked in the back door, the daughter was there to meet her with a big hug and a cup of tea to help her unwind from her first day back at work. She suggested to the mom that she go lie down on her bed and take a little nap, and she would wake her up when it was time to start dinner.

The mom was too tired to do anything else. She slipped off her shoes, put down her purse, took the cup of tea, and went in to lie down. This was perfect. Just the way the daughter had planned it. After about fifteen minutes, the daughter went to her own room where Bella was sleeping and gently woke Bella up to tell her who was home. Immediately, Bella began to purr loud and long. The daughter told Bella where the mom was and that now it was her turn to go tell the mom she was home.

The mom's bedroom door was cracked about six inches, just wide enough for Bella to go in. The mom always left it that way by habit so Bella or Mr. Kitty could come and go if they decided they wanted to. The mom had just laid her head on the pillow for a nap when she heard it the first time: *tinkle, tinkle*. She thought she was dreaming. Then she thought it was the kids next door playing outside because the window by the head of the bed was open. Then, just as she closed her eyes, she heard it again, *tinkle, tinkle*, but in a different place. This time, she knew it wasn't a dream. She lay still but with her eyes open, looking over at the edge of the bed. That's when she knew; the baby was home.

Bella tried to sneak up on the mom, but her bell gave her away. Mr. Kitty was thankful for the bell too! Now he would always know where Bella was when she was home.

The mom was so happy. Bella curled up right next to the mom in her favorite spot and purred louder than she ever had before. They spent the rest of the afternoon lying there together, telling each other all about their adventures in the last week until they both fell asleep. And that's how the dad found them when he came home from work. He wondered if the mom had found Bella yet; then he knew when he tiptoed into the bedroom and saw them snuggled up together.

The dad backed out of the room and closed the door. He thanked the universe for returning Bella to their family unhurt and safe. He had learned his lesson about taking responsibility for others. He also learned about forgiveness. This all could have been avoided if he had gotten Bella's nametags when he was supposed to and put them on her. He knew this probably wouldn't keep Bella from playing hide-and-seek, but at least now she would have a return address on her. Even if Bella hadn't learned her lesson, the dad had learned his. The universe is a strange and wonderful place, and now the smallest part of the universe has a bell. Everyone would sleep well tonight, especially Bella.

Here Come The Holidays Again

First comes the colors
In the trees.
Then the autumn winds
Bring them down with bluster and a breeze.
Spreading them out across streets and towns
Piling them high over lawns and eaves.
Until all the leaves are gone
And the trees are bare.
What beautiful love notes from the season.

Some of us take pause to go home.
To gather round our family tables
And bow our heads to share
In a Thanksgiving meal together
For all those who are able.
To give thanks for all the blessings
That we've received throughout the year
And our lifetimes...
Then sit down with family and friends to
Touch base eye to eye and heart to heart
At the family table for a Thanksgiving meal.
Having sometimes spent the year apart
To see and hear how everybody's doing
And how they feel,
As we all head towards another winter
And the end of another year.

Soon all the geese will be gone
And the air will be cold, crisp, and clear.
A sure sign that winter is coming

And soon will be here.
Lights and music will fill the air
And bring many colors
Into the moonless nights.
Voices will ring out here and there
To sing out and declare
That Christmas is coming
Bringing carolers and good cheer.

Children will make ready for presents and toys,
And look forward to Santa Claus
On Christmas Eve
To visit all good little girls and boys.
While parents give thanks
For the birth of Jesus
On Christmas Day,
For all those who believe.
Parents count their blessings
For another year gone by too soon
That Christ our Lord was born this day
A long, long time ago...
And one day He'll come back for us
Because the Bible tells us so.

Another December To Remember

Happy Holidays and Merry Christmas
Should echo the joy of the coming seasons.
But for many there's sadness and heartache
For those who have their reasons
That takes years to get over or erase.
For some forty years
Seems like a long time ago,
For others like only yesterday.
A hunting accident, a car wreck,
A heart attack away.
The news came in September,
Only three maybe four months to live.
This time the cancer was here to stay.
It would be another December to remember,
Another time to forget and forgive.
All the harsh words ever spoken.
All the wrong things ever done.
All the hearts that were damaged or broken.
All the hurts held by everyone.
It's harder to forget
When death comes calling
In the frigid darkness of the winters cold
That chills you to the bone.
To take from you your dearest ones
With only their names left carved in stone.
Of course we know
That they were more than that...
In our hearts we hold them dear.
It's the pain behind the Christmas tree

That reminds us that they're not here.
The long cold days of winter
The cold and rainy nights
Of the New Year.
Makes it harder to heal inside.
And every year when Christmas comes
With trees and carols
And all the pretty lights,
Only reminds us when they died.
It was forty-three years ago on Christmas day
My father passed away.
And now your mother
Is scheduled to leave us soon too...
Maybe over the holidays.
Seems like I just got Christmas back again
So I could spend it with you
Without any Christmas tears...
Now it's another Christmas to remember
Especially for your mother dear,
On Jesus's birthday in December.
Maybe peace on earth good will toward all
Will find its way toward us next year.
When Hark The Herald Angles will sing
To your momma sitting at the table
Having dinner with the King.

Shouting Sun Whispering Moon

Shouting sun bursts through the trees
In a brilliant crescendo of light.
Creating crisp dark shadows
Of detail and outline with ease
Erasing any traces of the night.
Shadows of images dancing their way
Across the morning dew.
Opposites of absolutes are reflections of the day
Of mirages just passing through,
Changing in their paths to suit the season
Changing their shape in front of you.
All the while watching in the afternoon sun
Is a crescent shaped pale half moon,
Whose whispering ways have already begun.
With tales of evening stars soon to come
While she patiently waits for
The setting sun to finish out his day.
As his shadows are growing longer
When his work is nearly done
And his light begins to fade,
Whispering moon has begun to swoon
Over promises shouting sun has made.
Like a bride on her wedding day,
As the beauty of his passion play unfolds,
Shouting sun begins to set in his glorious way
With crimson reds, violets and gold's
When he brings an end to another day.
While whispering moon has begun to whiten
Preparing for the night by

Lighting the stars along her way.
Greeting the clouds as they sail on by
Into the twilight and out of the day.
Whispering to the world as she puts it to sleep
Her lullaby lingers across the night,
Of her promises she prepares to keep.
Her moon shadows are quiet, soft and gray;
Her moonbeams subtle and white.
It's shouting sun that rules the morning
And whispering moon that rules the night;
Since the beginning of time it's been that way.
Sun shouts his glory into the morning
Moon whispers her peace
Into the night when we pray.
We bow our heads to the sun high above us,
Shade our eyes from his power and might,
Bare our bodies to the moon when we undress
And lift our eyes to her heavenly light.
Hot and scalding are sun's ultra violet rays
That turn your skin from white to red.
Cool and inviting is moon's mesmerizing gaze
And a beacon for lovers in the night, in their beds.
Our spirits rejoice under shouting sun
And our bodies under whispering moon.
Our secrets never told to anyone.
Shouting sun sees our truth at high noon

Without shadows for us to hide.
Whispering moon watches over us at night
And sees our passionate side.
Our promises may come to her
From out of the shadows
But our truths lay naked in her light.
Shouting sun brings me the morning.
Whispering moon brings me the night.
And in between is my life.
From beginning to end
They both are my friends,
This celestial husband and wife.
Shouting Sun king of the morning
Whispering Moon queen of the night.

Shouting Sun and Whispering Moon

This is the story of a little boy named Jason, and one day in his very busy life with two of his very special friends, Shouting Sun and Whispering Moon. Jason lives with his mom and dad, his dog, Ruby, and a cat named Buddy. It's a story about the sun and the moon and the imagination of a small boy who lives life in between the two of them in a very special way.

Shouting Sun burst into Jason's room through his window with such warm joy it's a wonder he didn't break the glass. He burst through Jason's curtains with sunshine joy, filling every crack and every opening with his light, searching Jason's bedroom, over covers and across stuffed animals, toys, and clothes, to find his little friend. In the quiet of the dawn, in the early morning hours, Shouting Sun reached up from the foot of Jason's bed in search of something familiar, something of his little friend to touch: an arm, a leg, a hand, or a foot. Slowly, Shouting Sun rolled his way up Jason's bed, searching for something to warm up to to let his little friend know that he was there. It was time to get up, time to come out and play.

Shouting Sun was getting worried. He had almost run out of bed to search, and still no sign of Jason! He was about to give up, when something moved, something stirred from under Jason's covers. As Shouting Sun neared Jason's pillow, he saw it. Just what he was looking for. It was something small but just enough. It was part of Jason to touch, to tell him that he was there.

There, beside Jason's pillow, just barely sticking out from under his covers, was one of Jason's ears. It was enough for Shouting Sun to touch, to warm, to shout to Jason that morning was here, and he should get up and start his day. As Shouting Sun rose higher in the morning sky, his enthusiastic glow began to warm Jason's covers where the boy's one little ear was showing.

The higher Shouting Sun rose in the morning sky, the warmer his enthusiasm got, and soon Jason began to warm and wake up as his curtains began to flutter from the warm air coming from out of the furnace vents right below. The curtains sent Shouting Sun's morning shadows darting and dancing all around Jason's room and across his pillow.

That's when Jason sat up! Now, Shouting Sun warmed Jason's pajama tops. With eyes closed, Jason smiled back at Shouting Sun while he finished waking up and thanked him for another sunny day. Jason loved the morning, and Shouting Sun's shadows were always entertaining as they moved across his room over his toys and up and down the walls.

He loved Shouting Sun and everything about him. It meant that morning had come, another day had begun, and he could get up and have breakfast. It meant that it would be warm and sunny outside today and maybe even hot, so he might not need a jacket. Maybe he could even wear shorts. It meant that the day would be full of light so he could play outside longer into the evening. When Shouting Sun filled the day, everybody was in a better mood. The plants and trees grew tall reaching for his loving rays.

Jason's dog, Ruby, loved chasing Shouting Sun's shadows over the sidewalk and across the fence, while Buddy the cat liked taking a nap in his favorite chair that Shouting Sun warmed up for him.

Now, Jason was awake! He bounded from his bed and across his room and out the door. His little feet pounded the floor in the hallway as he ran toward his parents' room to sound the alarm. When he got there, he flung open the door, and in two steps, he leapt up onto his parents' bed and said, "Rise and shine! Shouting Sun's up—let's have a hot pancake and an egg!" Jason's parents acted surprised, but they were already awake. They were familiar with Jason's sunny morning ritual and were ready and waiting for their little two-legged alarm clock to begin their day.

Jason loved the morning, and he especially loved the sunny days. He liked starting them early. It seemed to make them last longer that way. All day long, Jason would play outside with Shouting Sun. He helped his mom with the flowers, and he played with Ruby. He helped his dad wash the car and weed the yard, and then played hide-and-seek with Buddy whenever the cat was around.

Jason loved Shouting Sun for keeping him warm and dry so he could do all the things he loved to do outside that he couldn't do if it were raining. And at the end of every day, Jason sat in his favorite chair on the front porch to say good night to Shouting Sun and watch his beautiful sunsets. Every sunset was different and special and always full of color.

No matter where Jason was, he always tried to be outside or find a window to watch Shouting Sun's sunsets and say goodbye for the day, to thank him for his sunshine and watch him paint the sky for the night, setting the stage for Whispering Moon and her stars that would watch over him while he slept.

Jason loved Whispering Moon! But for different reasons. He loved her for her nightlight that helped him find his way around in the dark and not be afraid. He also loved her for her ability to change shape throughout the month. Jason loved Whispering Moon's faces, and that he could look directly at her without shielding his eyes for a long time. He was mesmerized by her beauty. It seemed to match her name, "Luna."

Whispering Moon loved Jason, and she followed him from room to room in his house, lighting his way in the night so he wouldn't be afraid of the dark. She even followed Jason in his parents' car when his family went out at night—always shining through his window, no matter which direction they went. She lit up Jason's seat over his shoulder to let him know she was there. On those special days during the month when Whispering Moon's face was the fullest, Jason's mother let him have a special treat. She would turn out the light in the bathroom and open the curtain across the window over the tub when Jason took his bath. While Jason played with his boats and toys, Whispering Moon flooded his tub with moonlight and painted his water with moonbeams.

Jason got to stay in his tub as long as it took Whispering Moon to pass by his window. This was their special time alone. But Jason's favorite time with Whispering Moon was when he said his prayers right before bed. His parents let him turn out the lights and open up the curtains while they stood in the doorway to watch. This is how Jason said his prayers every night. Then he thanked Shouting Sun and Whispering Moon for another beautiful day. When he was done, his mom and dad tucked him in and said good night.

Jason tried to stay awake and watch Whispering Moon through his window as long as he could before she moved on in her journey through the night, but he usually fell asleep before she was gone. He knew she would understand. He also knew that the sooner he fell asleep, the sooner he would see Shouting Sun and could start another day with his heavenly friends.

With Buddy asleep at the foot of his bed and Ruby on her rug beside him on the floor, Jason fell asleep—into the arms of the night behind Whispering Moon's nocturnal flight and on toward Shouting Sun's jubilant rise. Jason rested his tired eyes in dreams.

Furs And Purrs

If Zen where an object,
A being, a thing
With air in its lungs
And blood in its veins
Then certainly this being
So smug on my lap
Would have to be Zen
In the shape of my cat.
The master of breath,
Purring in purring out,
Is a living lesson to be learned.
With every breath,
Purring in purring out,
A blessing is born
And another moment to be alive is earned.
There's peace in breath
And breath in life
Wrapped up in those purrs and furs
Like lightning in a bottle.
Resting on my lap.
From paws to claws,
From still to full throttle,
From zero to instant in a flash!
All becomes one.
Nothing goes unnoticed
And nothing is left undone.
For my cat life is a series of moments

Wrapped up in purrs and furs.
To be lived between life and death.
Where blessings are reserved for the living
Purring in purring out
Until she takes her last breath.

Sweet Bones

She's six pounds
Of fur covered carcass
When she's sleeping
Or on the prowl
With a voice like broken glass
Across a chalk board.
You can tell where she is
When she's up and about
From her earsplitting screeching howl.
For twenty one years she's been killing
Everything that crosses her path
That walks, crawls, or flies,
But she's too old now
To go out hunting and chasing anymore.
If she's not sleeping or eating,
She's taking a bath!

She's a well-traveled girl
Having lived in all our houses.
Minded three dogs and tolerated two other cats.
Chased, killed and eaten many "mouses"
And she's still alive...
She's out lived them all.
She still goes out climbing and exploring
On occasion, but she always
Comes back when I call.
Her screech is louder than she weighs.
Her spirit is warm
Held against my heart.

It's the only thing she owns
That isn't broken or torn apart,
And I wouldn't trade it for time or gold.
She's the softest thing
I've ever loved
That's loved me back
With four paws
That I've ever known.
And when she's finally gone
I'll miss those mournful cries
And those warm caresses
From her sweet bones.

My Four-Legged Heart

My four legged heart
Looks up at me with brown eyes
And pours her self into my soul
While we share my morning coffee.
Her years are beginning
To show on her face and in her step.
We both know
Her journey is almost over.
All her love now
Is in her eyes.
No more running and chasing.
No more long walks
Beside river canals and mountain streams.
No more running on the beach.
She runs in her dreams now.
And waits for me
Patiently with loving eyes
To do what must be done.
My four-legged heart knows
When it's time to go.
And the hardest part
Of loving a dog
Is always the good bye.
Always....

Love Without Purpose

It's been a while
Since our last dog.
She was the smarter half
Of a loving set.
A sweet pair of springers:
Brother and sister, Ruby and Joe.
Through thick and thin, beginning to end,
Where one went the other
Was sure to go.
First two, then one, then none...
Eleven short years as a loving pair.
Then only two more
Loving a lonely one.
Until at last she too had passed
And was gone.
Leaving us without a purpose.
To love and be loved
By our dearest friends
Whose company was a joy to keep.
Walking or running for mile after mile
Or just curled up with them
While they sleep.
Now the only one left is their cat.
We share with each other
All we have left are her purrs,
And of course, my lap
To keep us from being lost.

Phil Pochurek

The Fourth Of July Tree

William Justice looked like an average boy. Twelve years old and about five foot six, he had average length blond hair, nicely trimmed about his collar, and a set of striking blue eyes that could hold your attention to the point of distraction. Of course, by then he knew he had you, and would politely blush and flash his million-dollar smile that absolutely no one could resist: a very handsome boy, destined for great deeds in the world, and certain to charm the socks off of everyone he met along the way.

Our story is about one of these deeds—a great accomplishment for anyone, young or old. Now, aside from William's all-American good looks, it was his name that stood out among his peers: "Justice."

The Justice family was the oldest name in town. In fact, the town of Independence was founded and built by them two hundred years ago. Branches of their family tree could be found all over town. You could mail a letter at the Abraham Justice Post Office, or apply for a marriage license at the Steven Justice Court House. After which, you could walk across the street and get a room at the Alexander Justice House, a grand three-story bed and breakfast run by William's parents and grandparents. Life had been peaceful and prosperous in Independence, ever since its beginning in the summer of 1776.

William's great-great-great-grandparents, William and Grace Justice, had sailed across the Atlantic from France and landed on the eastern shores of the Americas with very few belongings and all of their savings to start a new life in the New World. When their feet touched the soil of the New World after a long and nearly disastrous ocean crossing, they purchased a wagon and some horses and set out for the West. They were risking everything they had worked and saved for on the adventure of a lifetime. They had no maps, but they did have a compass to point them west toward the places they were going to, which were basically uncharted territories: a wilderness unknown, called New France. Occasionally, they were lucky enough to travel with someone who was headed in the same direction that they were and shared some of the same dreams that they had.

They journeyed westward on the crest of a Great Revolutionary War, leaving in their wake a battle for independence that would result in the birth of a new nation, the United States of America. These were exciting times, but these labor pains would not come without sacrifice. Brave men came forward under the threat of death, ready to back their beliefs and principles with blood if necessary. Life or death promises were made, that all men are created equal and deserve a life with liberty and justice for all, in their pursuit of happiness in these new United States. Powerful words to live by and in some cases die for.

William and Grace were proud to have come to America, even in the middle of this turmoil, to be a part of this dream, these new beginnings. They had been traveling west now since the spring of 1773. Across rivers and mountains, over the Great Plains and deserts. The things they saw and experienced and the people they met along the way (mostly Indians, the true Native Americans) were as spectacular and grand as they could have ever hoped for. The Justices were truly living their dreams.

By April of 1775, they came upon a small clearing along a river at the wide end of a long and beautiful valley, several months beyond the boundaries of New France. It was nestled between two mountain ranges, not far from the Pacific Ocean. They camped beside a river and rested the horses and their spirits. There was something special, sacred the Indians would later say, about the place where William and Grace decided to end their journey and make their home.

The Justices liked living by the river, and soon new people began arriving, a couple of wagons full a month or floating in on river rafts. Barges would later bring their supplies to them, along with any news of the war. It was the first of July, and the war, the battle for independence, which would last for eight long years, was underway.

William and Grace had staked out their homestead claim along the river just north of what had become a village. Six hundred and forty acres of rich farm land for growing grain, or grazing cattle, with plenty of forest to start building their dream, a town. A settlement where newcomers, pioneers like themselves, could settle down and raise families, build schools and churches, and practice the trades and skills they brought with them from the old world to this one.

It was a hot summer day, late in the afternoon on July 4, 1776. A family who traveled from the east had just arrived by barge with the news that on this day one year ago, July 4, 1775, a declaration of independence had been signed, declaring the thirteen colonies of the United States of America to be a free and sovereign nation. This was wonderful news, just what the Justices had been waiting for. They had been working from dawn to dusk building their dream, a town that they would call Independence in commemoration of this joyous moment in history, and paying tribute to the brave men who helped define the meaning of independence in their new United States, who signed their names to a declaration that they believed in their hearts to be true, even under the threat of death should they do so.

In a show of their support and in the spirit of the new nation, William and Grace planted a Douglas fir tree in what would later become the center of town. It was a seedling from one of the tallest fir trees that grew on the far western corner of their property—trees that would later build a post office, court house, and, of course, the Alexander Justice House. Those trees were the most magnificent trees William had ever seen. Twenty-five feet across at the base, some of them reached over one hundred eighty feet tall. William could think of no better symbol to represent this moment in history than to plant a seedling from a tree this grand that would one day grow into a living monument. The seedling William planted that day would grow to represent the dreams of a nation and all those who fought to make them come true.

From then on, the nation grew at a breakneck speed, and so did Independence. Once word had spread of the settlement on the river, people began to come. Every year on the Fourth of July, William and Grace would hold a grand party in the town square and also a sort of state-of-the-town meeting, ending with fireworks, a toast, and rededication of the town's living monument to freedom, the Douglas fir tree William and Grace had planted years before. As the town grew, this celebration became an Independence tradition, and the tree in the town square became known as the Fourth of July Tree. As the tree grew in size, so did the nation, adding stars to the flag for each new state in the union.

It was at one of these celebrations that Grace unveiled the latest flag with the newest addition of stars to its blue field atop its red and white stripes, representing the original thirteen colonies. The flag was glorious, and the tree seemed to sway in the afternoon breeze with its approval. It was at that moment when William and Grace's youngest son, Alexander, proposed the idea of mounting a flagpole atop the tree and flying the flag from there for all to see. A splendid idea thought William and Grace, as did all the town's people gathered for the celebration.

This was the beginning of a new tradition in Independence, that on the fourth day of July, the celebration and rededication of the tree would end with the changing of the flag. Once a year on that day a drawing would be held, and a winner would be chosen to climb up the tree and replace the old flag with the new one. On this day, July Fourth, 1786, Alexander Justice would be the first one to climb the tree, and his name would be engraved on a plaque that would later be hung on a wall in the entryway of the William Justice Court House in Independence. Now, at this time, the concern for a ten-year-old boy climbing a tree forty-five feet tall wasn't as great as it would become, where our story picks up today.

Independence is still a small town on a river, just like it always was, and of course William and Grace are long since gone, but their legacy lives on in the town they founded over two hundred years earlier. Most notably in Independence is the landmark Fourth of July Tree, standing tall now at two hundred feet to the top and twenty-five feet around at its base. A great and truly spectacular natural monument to our Independence. In the court house foyer is a brass and oak plaque with a list of all the names of those who have climbed the tree since the changing of the flag tradition began one hundred and ninety years ago. The list includes two US presidents, three congressmen, and five justices, who over the years proudly added their names to the list. Because of television coverage for the first time this year the changing of the Fourth of July Tree's flag could be watched throughout the nation and the world. Commemorating all those who had made the climb in the past.

This made young William proud to be a Justice. He had earned the respect of his family and his town, at his school with good grades, through his church with acts of kindness and devotion to others, and even to his country, now that he was about to add his name to the long list of others who had climbed the Fourth of July Tree for the annual changing of the flag. The mayor of Independence had pulled his name out of the Liberty cup, a large brass chalice that was used for this occasion.

William heard the news on his way home from the Alexander Justice House, where he worked the front desk in the summer months to supplement his allowance. So, on his way home, he stopped by the courthouse to check to see if his name was really on the list, and sure enough his name was at the top. There were always two names on the list just in case something happened to the first person chosen to make the climb before the dedication. In the history of the celebration, William could only remember one time when the original person chosen couldn't carry the flag. The day before, that person had broken his leg falling out of a tree practicing for the climb, so the first runner-up got to do the honors. But that was the last thing on William's mind.

He was so excited that he was chosen he could hardly wait to tell his parents, especially Grandpa who had made the climb seventy years before him, when he was William's age. It wasn't until he stepped outside the courthouse into the afternoon sun that he felt kind of light-headed but didn't become dizzy until he looked up at the Fourth of July Tree towering over him at a whopping two hundred feet. This tree inspired awe just being in its presence, especially now that he was about to become a part of its history too.

During his walk home, he wasn't quite sure how he felt. He was so excited to be chosen, and to add the Justice name once again to the oak and brass plaque in the courthouse. It was an honor and a chance to become a part of history, the chance of a lifetime, but something was wrong. Something wasn't quite right. William was forced to confront a secret known only to him: he had to face his greatest fear, his fear of heights, and he didn't know what to do. So many people would be counting on him. He had dreamed about this day, never giving it a thought that it really might come true, and now it was here and only a day away. The stage was being assembled in the town square around the base of the tree, and the grandstands were going up. Television crews were already in town and would soon be knocking on his door, for an interview with the all-American boy who would the climb the Fourth of July Tree.

When William got home, Grandpa was the only one in the house, and was waiting for him in the kitchen.

"How are you, William?" Grandpa asked. "Something wrong? You look a little peaked."

"I'm fine, Grandpa. I just got some great news. The mayor drew my name out of the Liberty cup to be the one to change the flag on the Fourth of July Tree."

"That's wonderful, William. Are you going to do it?"

He thought it was funny that Grandpa would even ask him such a question since he had never even heard of anyone turning down this honor after they had been chosen. "I think so, Grandpa. I'm still sort of in shock."

"Well, give it a little time to settle in, sleep on it. You've got a day to decide. Drink this glass of Grandma Justice's herbal tea before you head up to your room. It'll give you strength and help you make the right decision."

Grandpa's words and matter-of-fact attitude had a strangely calming effect on William as he went upstairs to his room. His room was at the west end of the house, and out his window was a perfect view of the town square and, of course, the Fourth of July Tree, with last year's flag flying proudly in the afternoon sun for the whole town to see. He lay back on his bed, trying to picture himself at the top of the tree. It was swaying in the breeze as he reached for the flag to change it, with the whole world watching, when he closed his eyes.

It was July Fourth and the parade had just begun on First Street. It would end at the Town Square, circle around the Fourth of July Tree, and finish in the field behind the grade school across the street, where camera crews and news media had set up their equipment to record and broadcast this monumental event.

William was to ride on the last float and hold a pole waving the flag that he would take up the tree to exchange for the flag put there the previous year. The parade had been going for half an hour when his float finally took off, with him perched on top, holding a ten-foot flagpole with the famous flag. It was beautiful, with bright colors. The flag was four times the normal size so it could be seen from everywhere in Independence. It was made out of some space-age fabric that could take the exposure of the year-round weather in Independence. Wind, rain, sun, and ice. It was water repellant and UV protected. Things had really changed since William and Grace had started this tradition some one hundred and ninety years before.

The Justices never could have imagined that their ceremony would become a national event, worldwide even. Through all the flags and the ones who climbed up to change them over the years, how the tree had flourished—standing tall and proud, just like William knew it would, gladly offering its limbs to all those who had climbed before. The tree grew taller year after year as if in tribute to its job, curator of the symbol of our nation swaying in the wind for everyone to see.

Young William was still staring up at the tree when the float stopped and the fireman called for him to come down so he could begin his climb up. The crowd was cheering and waving little American flags and shouting his name. It all seemed like a blur as he stepped into the bucket of the extension ladder on the biggest fire truck Independence had, which would lift him up to the lowest branches of the tree to begin his climb. Even those were fifty feet off of the ground now. As the ladder reached its fullest extension, the fire chief who was alongside William folded and placed the flag in a canvas saddlebag that was hand signed and dated by everyone who had made the climb before him. He handed William a pen so he could add his name to the bag, which was part of the tradition. William's hand was shaking a little by the time he finished signing the date. He tossed the strap over his shoulder so both of his hands would be free to climb. The fire chief opened the safety latch on the extension ladder bucket, and then shook his hand. He wished William luck and said he was proud to shake the hand of the one who would be changing the flag, and before he let go, he looked William straight in the eyes and asked him if he was sure he wanted to go through with it. At that moment, time stood still. This was William's last chance, one final opportunity to change his mind. He hesitated a moment, but in that instant he knew; he not only saw all of those who had climbed before him, but he saw the fifty-six men who signed the Declaration of Independence on this day two hundred years ago, standing on the courthouse steps, watching and waiting for him to begin. He said, "Yes," and then he stepped from the bucket and grabbed the first branch to begin his climb.

    He climbed a few branches and looked back at the bucket receding toward the ground to the cheers of "William Justice for all." It was a chant that became his mantra as he climbed, careful only to look where he was going, and not where he had been. The tree was truly magnificent as he climbed, and the closer he got to the top, the more it felt like he was going back in time. All of the limbs that were so graciously aiding in his ascent represented a different space in time, a new era. The things this tree had seen.

As he got closer to the top, the trunk narrowed, and he was more aware of how much the tree was swaying from side to side, about six feet. Instantly, his hands began to sweat from fear. The fear that he had managed to overcome began to gnaw at the pit of his stomach, until he froze. Unable to move in either direction, he was realizing a terror greater than he had ever known in his life. The trunk of the tree was probably only three feet around now and the branches were much smaller too, but easier to hold in his vice-like grip. He looked up and could just make out the flagpole ahead of him about twenty feet. The crowd had become silent now, sensing that something was wrong. This only made things worse, because with their silence went his strength; their chant, his mantra, "William Justice for all," had stopped. He closed his eyes and held on for life, his life, completely engulfed by his greatest fear. It seemed like an eternity. The firemen were getting ready to start climbing up to rescue him, when he heard it again, "William Justice for all!" He opened his eyes and took a deep breath—the air was fresh and smelled sweet like the forest—and he relaxed his grip for a minute. Then he heard it again, "William Justice for all," only one voice, but it sounded familiar, enough so that he managed to look down to see his Grandpa standing in the bucket of the fire truck waving his hat and shouting "And William Justice for all." Soon others joined in, and the chant was even louder than before. He took another breath and reached for the next branch and said to himself, "And William Justice for all." He grabbed the next branch, to the wild cheers of the crowd below. The tree trunk was only eighteen inches around now; he reached for the flagpole to unsnap the cable from the pulley the flag was on and lower it to within his reach. He let out a cheer, "WAHOOOO." He had won. He had faced the enemy on its ground and conquered his fear. Even if he was the only one who knew there was a battle being fought, he had won. He unsnapped the flag from the pole that it had been tethered to for a full year of outstanding service to Independence, and this country; its job was done. He reached into his bag, unfolded the new flag, and carefully snapped it into place while a drumroll pounded the sky from below. After he had secured the new flag in its place, he set it free in the afternoon breeze, the sun shining off its new colors. That was the signal for the Independence High School Marching Band to start playing the "Star Spangled Banner." Slowly, he raised the flag to its new resting place to begin its yearlong tour of duty. He raised his arm and waved to everyone down below. He could see his house in the distance, and he stopped for a moment when he realized that someone was looking at him with binoculars from his window and waving. He strained to see who it was when a sign dropped down from his window that read, "You did it! William Justice for all." It was Grandpa, waving and cheering, then holding his arm, "William, William, wake up!" William opened his eyes and sat up on the edge of the bed. It was sunset now as he looked across the town toward the tree, with half a dozen giant spotlights shining on the flag flying at its very tip. He was wringing wet from sweating but felt somewhat relaxed after having been through what he thought he had just done. Grandpa just smiled and said, "I knew you could do it! I had the same problem you did when it was my turn to make the climb seventy years ago, and I knew no one would understand. I saw it on your face this afternoon when you came home, so I decided to help you through it, just like my grandfather helped me, through your dreams. Then I made you a gift of love and hope, wrapped it in courage, and you washed it down with Grandma's iced tea this afternoon.

It's an old Justice family remedy. It helps you sleep so you can work things out where it's safe, and when you wake up everything is okay. It was all you, William; you did it yourself, just like I did and all the other Justices did who made the climb before you. Now come downstairs and eat; everybody's waiting for you to begin the party. You've got a big day ahead of you tomorrow, William, and tomorrow is your day."

He didn't know how to explain it, but it all seemed so natural, almost supernatural, but whatever Grandma and Grandpa had done, it had worked. He went downstairs and out to the backyard to where the family celebration party in his honor was about to begin. The house was full of Justices. They joked about it and called it the Supreme courtyard. There were five Justices in all who had made the climb, including Grandpa, who was the oldest Justice still living to make the climb, and they were all there. They brought their flags and pictures along with their stories of the fateful day that they made their climbs. Though all the stories had a personal twist, they all shared a common thread; they all had a deathly fear of heights. None of them mentioned or told anyone about it either, until the next Justice was chosen to make the climb. With the telling of each story, William felt his fear slipping further and further away, and himself coming closer and closer to the bond that united them all, the founders of the legacy, William and Grace Justice: two people who shared a dream and followed it to a place on a river, and a town they would build together and name Independence. They would plant a tree that would grow into the hearts of everyone in this great nation—a nation that was about to celebrate its bicentennial, and William Justice would climb the Fourth of July Tree into the history books, becoming a part of its living legacy. Tomorrow, there would be a "William Justice for all," and he was ready.

Looking Down

He never saw it coming.
He never heard a sound.
He never heard the shouts and screams
"Look out!" "Look up!" "Turn around!"
He had his ear buds in.
He was looking down.
He never played ball,
Rode a bike, or learned to swim.
"You could get hurt!" "You could drown!"
Life in the real world scared him.
So he started looking down.
Games and Podcasts filled his eyes and ears.
Then Instagram and selfies
Used any time that was left.
His hands never touched a book.
They said he was advanced for his years.
He could multitask with the best of them;
He was a genius to his peers,
But never really got anything done.
His life was one big Instagram
So he was always on the run.
And for all that time lost while he played
He paid the ultimate price,
With the last step he would ever take.
And with that step he scored an extra life!
It would be his last mistake.
Too bad he couldn't use it now
To save him in real life!
He'd never been on an airplane,
But in one step he was about to fly.

The car that hit him
Shot him thirty feet in the air;
Sent him a hundred feet down the road
And gave him his last look up at the sky.
The bone crushing impact was instantaneous.
He never really felt any pain.
One moment he was locked
In mortal combat with Xanos,
The next he would never breathe again.
Everyone stopped for a moment
While they came to take him away.
The few that stopped took pictures,
But had nothing to say
As he lay there on the ground.
The rest that passed by didn't notice...
They were busy looking down.

A Road To Nowhere

When pride becomes anger
And violence strikes out in fear,
In an instant all ground that was gained is lost.
You can taste the electricity in the air
When sparks go flying
And words become visceral,
Cutting and slashing anyone who is near
That engages them so all dialogue is lost.
Faces and names get lost in the rage;
It's the cost we pay when we're there.
There's nothing more to understand.
Nothing you can say that's right
No mater how much you care.
No sense can be made when
Every word is a struggle and ends in a fight.
When all memory is lost with no end in sight,
And that's only the beginning of the end.
When the lucid distraction of common ground
Always seems to be just around the bend.
But every time you reach that turn
Something goes south, goes sideways again,
And they're blinded with anger
As they begin to slip
Back to where reality is just a memory
For those caught in dementia's grip.
Don't engage or you'll just enrage
Unless it's a risk you want to take.
Be loving, kind, and strong in your care

But don't make that mistake.
Remember they've forgotten more than you may know
And going home is all they want to do
Even when there's nowhere left to go,
And the person who looks like someone
You once knew isn't even there.
Heading down a road to nowhere
Until all that's left is despair.

When the days of fighting are over
And there's no screaming
And shouting anymore
Just eating and sleeping all day long
With no memory from the moment before,
Something is terribly wrong.
How could something like this happen?
To the ones we hold so dear.
Lost in their dementia until their gone
Never satisfied with just being here.
Always trying to go home again
To a home they'll never see.
Heading down a road to nowhere,
Hanging on to a memory,
Of a home that isn't there anymore
And never will be...

No More

No more stressful nights without sleep,
No more doctors appointments to keep,
No more calls to 911,
Grandma's job is over and done.
Her life long journey had come and gone.
No more fights over what she did
No more apologies for what she said
No more long days sleeping in bed
Grandma's time had come.
No more fights over what to eat
No more promises to try and keep
At last a rest and peaceful sleep.
No more medicine to sort and take
No more forgetting no more mistakes
No more meals to try and make
Now we're on our own.
Her pain and suffering has gone away
The good Lord saw to that today
When He came and took her by the hand
To lead her to the promise land
And be at his side.
No more pain for her to take
No more hiding her mistakes
I'm glad she's finally at rest.
And know she's in God's loving hands
Her life on this earth is through.
In loving memories I think of her
Whenever I'm with you.

Pink Slips

We all dread them.
Some of us have gotten one
And some of us choose one.
One can put and end
To our work life, our job.
The one that gives us
Our room and board.
But the one that we choose
And put on our fridge
Comes at the end of our life.
And tells the ones who
Who come to save us no thank you,
We've already been saved by the Lord.
When our bodies are worn out
Our lives are full
And our cup runneth over with love
And all that's left are our habits,
We're tired at the end
Of a life long journey
And looking like velveteen rabbits.
When all our chores are done,
Our children are raised
And our oldest friends
Have mostly gone on ahead,
Who wants to hang around
And wait for a broken hip?
Sign the love letter
That's posted on your fridge

That says you're right with the Lord,
And when that day finally comes
You'll be ready to jump ship.
It's posted right there on the fridge...
Signed and dated on your pink slip.

In The Rain

In the rain the ocean roars again,
Pours again its endless tides
Down and over everything it touches
Over everything that resides under the sky.
Washing over all creation turning it green,
Making it clean and fresh so all its colors
Can be seen with the naked eye.
Each rain drop makes a sound in symphony
When they hit the ground
Your roofs, the streets, a timpani—
Against your window panes, its steady beats
Filling gutters dripping off the eaves
Rushing and swirling towards every drain
Pouring over every rock, over all the leaves
The same on its way back
To the sea from where it came.
In the rain the ocean whispers a dream
Nourishing everything seen and unseen
And everything in between earth and sky
It's rhythm a song a lullaby
A promise to every seed to grow.
In the rain the color of life is green;
To the ocean it's all just part of the show.
In the rain our tears join with the sky
To heal our hearts as we grow
Then cover for us when we cry
In the rain.

The Year They Left The Lights Up

Once there was a time when you could give someone a present, a gift, for no other reason than you love them. Not just for their birthday, Valentine's Day, a wedding, Christmas, or any reason that might imply an obligation, a hint of any return kind of gesture. A time when a gift was pure in intent, when all it required was to be received—a continuous and complete circle of love. Not a gift to show appreciation, gratitude, or reward, nothing as conventional as that, rather more natural, more a part of the person. A gift so simple, so pure no one realizes that it is one. Those are the best kind, the ones that we share every day. They begin with a smile, a laugh, or a compliment (things you should never keep to yourself). Watch the gifts grow from there, blossom from a kindness into a wonderful joy. That is what this story is all about.

It all started on the Saturday after Thanksgiving in a small town called Promise, population 329, give or take an occasional new baby. The first thing I noticed, when I got old enough to notice, was there were never any accidents in Promise, at least not any fatal ones.

Everyone who died lived a full life, happy and productive. They always seemed to know when their time was near, telling their children to send out invitations, and a Threshold party would be held. A sort of re-birthday party, a farewell gathering for everyone they could recall who had touched their lives in some way. Everyone was invited to come, count the blessings they recalled, and say their goodbyes.

This was a joyous occasion. People came from all walks of life, from near and far, to see their friends and relatives for one last time, to relive old times and share one last supper. A Thanksgiving of friends to one another, the final chapter of this life's journey before they departed for the next one.

George Stanton, a widower and retired schoolteacher, was the town's oldest living resident. It seems that everyone in town had passed through George's classroom at one time or another, so it was fitting that when he had his Threshold party, everyone in town was invited. All 328 of them.

Now George lived in a fine old two-story house, right downtown, that he built himself. It had lots of windows and rooms. The whole downstairs was one huge room with a fireplace at one end and a kitchen at the other. George loved to cook as much as he loved the people he cooked for; however, he hated being in the kitchen away from all of his guests, so he made his front room a sort of big kitchen, serving up soup and stories to anyone who would listen. Sooner or later, everyone in town ended up at George's for a meal and a tale of how the town of Promise had come to be. Most of them were still living in town, doing the same things their mothers and fathers had done, and even some of the things George had taught them: skills, trades, arts and crafts, and the stuff of life it takes to get by. Some left and journeyed out into the world. And some returned, disappointed that the rest of the world wasn't like Promise. When they came home, George was always there to welcome them back with open arms, a patient ear, a warm fire, and a full refrigerator. Because he loved to cook, there always seemed to be something just out of the oven or on the stove that you could smell for three blocks away. You could find George's house by following your nose, which is just what I did.

I was helping him get rid of some of his Thanksgiving leftovers, of course, so they wouldn't spoil. He had all the traditional treats: turkey, stuffing, sweet potatoes, cranberries, and pumpkin pie. It was all there. George and I had a great relationship; he loved to cook and tell stories as much as I loved to eat and listen. He chewed the fat, and I chewed whatever he gave me.

After my second and last piece of pumpkin pie, I reminded him it was time to get out his Christmas lights. His was a cherished and wonderful collection that sparkled and shown like an electric rainbow, and because his house was perched on the only hill in Promise, it could be seen from any direction in town. George was proud of his lights that he added to over the years, brightening up the holidays in Promise and reminding people that Christmas was coming.

It took some work, but two years ago, I finally convinced George to let me help put up his "Electric Birthday Candles" as he called them. George was a hard sell, but he eventually agreed he was too old to be climbing ladders. I told him by the time he got all of his lights up without falling, Christmas would be over anyway. We both laughed, and then I pointed out that I was too young to be hanging the lights up myself, unless he held the ladder for me.

So we had a deal. I did the climbing, and he did the ladder holding. And the lights went up. Everywhere. All around the windows, across the gutters, and down the rainspouts. It was a sight to behold when we were finished. George was proud of our work, proud that he had let me be part of something that meant so much to him. He considered his house to be a birthday card to Jesus, and he had let me sign my name on it. I didn't know at the time this would be George's last Christmas, until I got home and found my invitation to his Threshold party on my desk.

I thought about the times in class when he had told a story, taken the time to explain a piece of history, helped us learn how to solve a problem in math or life in general. I couldn't wait to go to school to see George and show him what I had learned and ask him for more. His cup was always full, and I was always thirsty for whatever he was pouring. He gave to us willingly, but never more than we could swallow at one time. He was an unending source of information and inspiration. And now he was leaving. How would Promise, or the world, get along without him? There was not a doubt in my mind that the world would be a lesser place without George Stanton, but also far richer for all the lives he touched and strengthened. I was glad for the times in the past few years that he had let me do things for him that he could no longer do for himself: mow his lawn, wash his car, weed and water his garden. All these things he took great pride in doing, but it hurt him now, so he was forced to let them go one by one. That's where I came in. It gave me great joy to take over these duties plus anything else I could think of to help him through his daily routine. When he tried to pay me for my help I laughed, then politely refused. I could never take money from someone who had given me so much. I considered it a privilege to finally give him something back. So we worked out a trade: "tales for toil," with an occasional sandwich thrown in. George taught me the gift of giving, and in return we both received from it, only now he was leaving. My best friend, my mentor, was having a Threshold party.

    The days before Christmas seemed to fly by, and soon school was out once again for the holidays. I was thankful for that because it meant that I could spend more time with George and help him get ready for his Threshold party.

    It was hard not to be sad. He could always tell when I was upset because I would get really quiet and I wasn't very hungry. This was a dead giveaway for George, so when it happened, he started telling me one of his Threshold stories. He recounted a tale of someone who had touched him, and how they had made a difference in the way he looked at life. These stories always seemed to distract me from the moment, just long enough to forget the fact that George would be leaving soon, but I could see how excited he was to be stepping across the Threshold from this life to the next, joining all of his friends who had gone before him. Of course, all this talk of his trips and new adventures always made me hungry.

That's when he knew he had succeeded. It made him happy to make someone feel good, and if he could get you to eat something he made, he was in heaven—a place George was soon to be, hopefully without having to do as much cooking and serving, a place where he could finally relax. That would be something new for George. At last he could enjoy a George just being, and not so much a George always doing. A sort of doing vacation, and he was ready.

He would probably still make his way to a kitchen eventually though. You could take George out of the kitchen, but you could never take the kitchen out of George. Christmas came at last, and it seemed as if there was a never-ending parade of people through George's house. The phone was ringing with people who couldn't make it to Promise this Christmas. Everyone else who was able came to see him, shake his hand, give him hugs, and hear one more story. George was overwhelmed and happy, reminding everyone to come to his Threshold party. They said they would, with a big smile, hoping that it would hide how much they were going to miss him and his stories, not to mention his famous, delicious soups.

It was on the eve of George's Threshold party, nearing the end of my holiday vacation, when I stopped by to see how he was doing and ask him when he wanted to take down his Christmas lights for the last time. He was sitting by the fireplace in his favorite chair, watching the flames dance on some distant shore. He didn't even notice when I came in and sat down next to him. Several minutes passed until the fire popped and startled him into looking my direction. He smiled and asked if I had been there very long. I said no, and asked if he needed anything done before his party, and when he would be ready to take down his precious lights. He sat quietly for a moment, smiled, and said, "Everything for the party is a go; as for the Christmas lights, I have decided to leave them up."

George never had any children. His wife passed away early in their marriage, before he came to Promise. He considered all of us, the people of Promise, his children.

He had managed to save a considerable amount of his teacher's pension since his retirement and had made some wise and very profitable investments over the years, creating the nice monthly income needed to buy groceries to feed everyone during his soup and story sessions. All things considered, he had decided to leave his house open to the people of Promise to use for a gathering place. It would be a place to hold town meetings and celebrations, but most of all, Threshold gatherings for the people of Promise. He told me that he had enough money in his savings account to pay the taxes on his house for many years and had set up a special account just for that. He also had accounts to pay the utilities: water, garbage and sewer, but most of all, the electricity. So his precious electric rainbow birthday card to Jesus could stay lit all year long, lit up to remind people that the spirit of giving shouldn't be tied to any one season or event, but should be carried in their hearts every day. George seemed to glow when he was telling me this, at the thought that his electric birthday card was going to stay lit year round. Not just for one holiday, but every day. It would signify that in Promise, all were welcome in his house.

The reason he was telling me this was that he wanted me to look after his lights, to care for them as long as I lived in Promise. I told him it would be a labor of love, just as it had always been, and I would consider it an honor to be the keeper of the lights. I promised to do my best to make sure that everything stayed just as it was. He smiled and thanked me. Others had requested various jobs to help out and be a part of the legacy of Promise House. This was a perfect tribute to George; he handed me a copy of his last wishes, his farewell gift to the town of Promise. I was honored he chose me to be the keeper of the lights. George was my best friend, and he knew I wouldn't let him down. He knew I loved his lights just as much as he did. It was a load off his mind and heart to know that his simple gift of love would go on, perhaps even to generations to come. I could tell that the excitement of the Promise House was taking its toll on George's eyelids. I suggested a nap, and George agreed.

He said he would see me tomorrow at his Threshold party, where he would tell everyone his plans. After they had eaten and run out of stories, before the goodbyes, he would tell them one last story, giving them his farewell gift.

I said goodbye to him, and he smiled and waved back. Then he said a hearty thank-you for loving his lights as much as he did (and for giving him my ultimate gift, my friendship) and that he would see me again at the party.

That was the last time I saw George. He went inside and sat in front of the fire, propped his feet under his favorite blanket, and began the journey to his next life.

I wished I would have known I was at his Threshold party when I was there, but I'm not sure I would have acted any different. It was nice having George to myself. I guess that's how he wanted it all along, nothing out of the ordinary, just him and me. I didn't find out until sometime later that I was the only one who got an invitation to his Threshold party. Right after I left, he phoned his doctor and left a message on his answering machine inviting him by in the morning for coffee. He did the same thing at the mayor's office at City Hall.

The next day, George's doctor arrived, along with the town elders. They found him in the chair, blanket and all, right where he was when I left him. Just the way he wanted it. He knew the doctor and elders would know what to do and left instructions with the last details to be attended to on the table beside his chair. He said he wanted to be cremated and his belongings given to those who had expressed a desire to have them.

Now George was a simple man and didn't have a lot of valuable possessions, mostly just the necessities. He considered his friends his most valuable possessions. Of all the things he did own, or ever expressed having any pride in owning, the most important were his Christmas lights. Those he left to me.

When I arrived that afternoon for George's party, his house was full. Some were laughing, some were crying, and everyone was eating. The whole town was there and not a single face I didn't recognize. Everyone made themselves right at home, as usual. It seemed like a Threshold party, except for one thing, someone was missing. I realized by the time I made my way from one end of George's front room to the kitchen and back, that he wasn't anywhere to be found. George was the one who was missing. As I walked around the room, every conversation, every story being told, was about him. No wonder I hadn't missed him quite yet. It was just as if he were still there, and that's the way he wanted it. I wandered around the room, a cup of soup in hand, and listened. Some of the stories were his stories; some of them I'd never even heard. Time seemed to stand still, and every so often I swore I caught a glimpse of him around the room among his friends. He was laughing and listening right along with them, only he *wasn't* there, he was gone. He was really gone this time. George had moved on—finally crossed his Threshold to a new life while the rest of us celebrated, remembered, and cherished the time he spent with us and thanked him for his gifts of life and love.

As the party began to wind down, people were talking less and were looking at all the pictures covering the walls. The pictures were years of memories, a lifetime of George's love captured in the moment and saved forever. I made my way to the front of the room by the fireplace, raised my glass of lemonade, and proposed a toast to my best friend.

"To George Stanton, my best friend, who touched all of our lives as if he were King Midas himself, only leaving us all the richer for having been touched by him. With his wit, his wisdom, and his love, he touched all our lives and changed us forever. May his memory live on in Promise, in our hearts, and in this house."

"Thank you, George. I'm proud to have known such a person as you and can only hope to have made as many friends as you have. We are all gathered here tonight to say thank-you and goodbye. Goodbye George, we love you."

After everyone had tipped their glasses to George, I invited them outside on the lawn to admire his Christmas lights. It was here I passed on his final wishes. His lights would stay up all year, in celebration of Jesus's birthday. They would mark not only the day that Jesus was born, but that He was given to us as the ultimate gift. George's gift to me was his Christmas lights, and I had been given the job of taking care of them. Everyone smiled and laughed and said that it was just like George to do something like that, but that they liked his idea, and most of all they liked his lights and their message. The lights reminded everyone of him and his true heart.

Then, slowly, as the New Year rolled around, things started getting back to normal in Promise. Kids went back to school, and when the holidays were over, a strange but wonderful thing started to happen. At a time when people would normally start taking down their Christmas lights and storing them for the next year, people left them up. All over town, lights were left up and turned on every night, in the spirit of Christmas, in memory of George. Several weeks had passed, and then months and everyone's lights were still up, only it didn't seem so strange anymore. In fact, it seemed quite normal and uplifting; every night Promise seemed to glow. People who didn't even have lights up during the holidays were putting them up. George had succeeded beyond his dreams. He had not only made his house a birthday card to Jesus, but the whole town of Promise, and not just for a couple of weeks over the holidays, but for the whole year.

To this day, when you look down on Promise from the surrounding hills, it sparkles like a jewel in the night, with George's house in the middle of it all. The city twinkles like an electric rainbow, carrying the spirit of Christmas, and George, along with the people's hearts it touches one day at a time, all year long, forever.

Love From Behind The Mask

As we move forward
In these uncertain times ahead
We've become avatars of our true selves.
Hidden from behind our masks
Surrendering our identities to the virus
In our common defense.
As we move forward
Out into a new version of our old world
And try to resume our old tasks
A new familiar is on the rise.
At home we reach out
Through FaceTime and Instagram
To touch each other and be close
From the inside out, in spirit only.
A digital form of love to reach out to everyone
To keep us from being lonely,
As we try to learn from our distant past
On our path as we move forward,
So we don't make the same mistakes
We did last time a pandemic struck.
Use our minds to turn the tides of disease
With science and medicine instead of luck.
Our nation together in sickness and in health
Until death do us part...
We shall overcome, we shall overcome.

Through lack of knowledge
And at great expense
We suffered through the tragedy of a lifetime
While the world was at war.

We fought with what we had
Against what we didn't know—
And almost lost.
Lessons learned and etched in time
For all to see how bad it can get
That ignorance has a price
And what it cost.
And now it's time has come again
To see if we've learned anything
From all those who went before.
With all we've come to know
From all the years that have passed,
Here we are once again
Living behind the mask
With a chance to get it right.
Everyone must work together
If we're going to win this fight,
Without suffering our past all over again.
Opening our hearts and using our minds
To do whatever it takes to win.
This is our time to listen and wait.
Be strong and patient to survive.
Let medicine rise up to meet the task.
Reach out from the inside through your eyes
To show your love from behind the mask.

Alone Together

We gather together
From behind all our screens
Safely disinfected from the pandemic.
Using time as a weapon,
Our sword and shield as a means,
Hope and faith to keep us
From becoming polemic.
In the beginning
Our arrogance became complacent
And fell like a new spring rain,
"We're too strong to get sick
And our scientists too wise,"
It was a familiar American refrain.
But it wasn't long before we noticed
How sick we had become
And the waters began to rise.
The enemy had invaded our lands.
It was too late now to point any fingers;
Our future had a number and a new name.
People were dying right before our eyes
We'll look back later to assign the blame...
The waters were rising and
There was nothing we could to do
But stay home and keep washing our hands.
We were deaf when we should have been listening.
Too blinded by our screens to see
That the waters were rising again but this time
They were coming for you and me.
Who could we look to to save us now

While we shelter in place from inside?
Where we've painted ourselves in a corner
Standing over an empty bucket of pride
While we wait for it to dry.
Now we're all painfully aware of the minutes
That fill the long hours in a day.
Confined to our homes like prisoners
Washing our hands, from a distance, while we pray.
Maybe now with all this time
We'll learn to listen.
Open our eyes and begin to see
That we're all in this boat together,
Sink or swim is up to you and me.
And the water is rising fast.
We can rise to meet the occasion
Or fall like the ones who have already passed.
It's a choice now we all get to make.
Saving others by saving ourselves first
Or keep making the same mistakes.
Now it's time for us to make some decisions
Like we've never before had to make,
While the fate of our lives is still in our hands.
Help the ones who are the weakest
Whenever wherever we can
Or paint a red banner over our door...
And hope for the best.
We're all in this alone together
With nothing but time on our hands

Phil Pochurek

So take this time to listen to your heart.
Tell everyone you know that you love them
That's the first place we all should start.
Then take a good long look in the mirror
And think about what you see.
After all the years you've been looking at them
Are they the person you hoped they would be?
There's so many questions we should be asking.
Maybe it's time to make a list
While we have all this time on our hands.
Thank the Lord and count our blessings,
Alone together as we shelter at home in place.
"Tell everyone you know how much you love them."
"We'll get through this alone together...
Stay home, wash your hands,
Don't touch your face."

A New Normal

How do we decide to do
Something that we've always done
As if it were something new?
Keeping our distance
From someone we love or anyone
Will be more challenging too!
No more handshakes when we meet.
Wiping down tables and chairs
Before we sit down to eat.
Wearing gloves and using towels
Going in and out of doors,
Something we've never had to do before
Is now an unspoken law.
Wearing masks and rubber gloves
As we go out into our day
And back to the lives we knew,
Is something we never did only months ago
But something we've all learned to do.
It's a brand new normal for each of us
For the lives we all once knew.
It's dangerous now to do the simplest of things
That everyone use to do.
Now we wash our hands and cover our faces
Everywhere we go whenever we go outside
To keep us safe and well
Ignoring these rules has consequences
And can be seen in the numbers
Of those who have passed on and died.

We're all in this together every single one.
We all want our lives back
The ones that we knew.
And that will depend on
The steps we take as we go back
To all the things we use to do.
Masks and gloves may be with us for a while
As we go out into our day.
The saddest part is that no one can see your smile
When they hear you say "thank you."
So we must learn to smile with our eyes!
To all those we see as we go out
And back to the lives we knew.
That we are who we are
From the inside out
And not defined by what we do.
As we learn a new way to see.
Never before have words meant more
Then coming from behind our masks
To whatever our new normal may be.

Phil Pochurek

Uncertain Times

We've seemed to have forgotten
How fragile we are
Living behind our screens.
Life is dangerous out there in the land of Oz.
Our ability to communicate
With someone around the world in seconds
Has by far exceeded our means.
We can go from Africa to Amsterdam
With the touch of a finger
Or the blink of an eye
Before we even put on our jeans
Without even leaving our homes.
We can order our food and water,
Have all our groceries delivered too,
It's no wonder we feel so alone,
But as humans some of us need to touch.
The youth these days
Move too fast for a hug
And others not so much.
Except to the door when their food has arrived.
Thank God someone else knows how to drive!
But out there waiting in the real world
On the other side of the screen
In the light of day is life and death.
People getting sick getting other people sick
With a fever and shortness of breath.
Too late to get ready for the storm.
Too many people are just working

And working their lives away.
Too busy taking pictures
And watching their screens
To hear what the world has to say.
Now it's too late to say we're sorry,
Too late to run and hide,
When so many people are getting sick
And too many others have already died.
Who do we go to for the answers?
About a virus in search of a host.
Who can we trust to tell us the truth?
It's the old and the sick that are dying now,
Until it comes back for our careless youth.
Indestructible from behind their screens,
How clear this cautionary tale has been
As an end to our millennial means.
Wash your hands, don't touch your face,
Stay at home and shelter in place, stay in.
They're going to pay everyone to watch TV.
It doesn't get much better than that!
Divide and conquer isolate and win!
While trying not to get too fat!
Look out for one another from behind closed doors.
How did we get to where we are?
I didn't go to China, New York, or Rome!
And I wash my hands frequently!
Hell, I never even left my home!
Now my new best friend is my car.

I cover my mouth when I cough and sneeze.
But apparently, we can shed
This virus just by talking
When we pass each other in the afternoon breeze.
In the beginning people wondered
If they might get it.
When the numbers began to go up.
Now we don't wonder if but when...
And we pray for a vaccine to save us
Before we become a number like so many of them.
But someday this will all be over
And all the numbers will even out,
When a new vaccine comes to save the day.
And all of those who made it through
Will wonder what this was all about.
Only nothing will ever be the same.
Remember, for all those people
Touched by the virus
That every number had a name.
So when all the numbers start coming down
And the deaths begin to subside,
Count your blessings to be one of the living left
When you're praying for all those who have died.

Nut Ratz

In and out
And up and down,
Across the street
And all around.
A straight line
Never happens
Until it's in front
Of your car...
Always running but
Never far from a tree.
Climbing and jumping
That's what they do
And who they are!
Above you, behind you, beside you,
In front of you.
Always running from dogs and cats!
Crazy, furry, chirping...
Nut ratz.

Leg Love

Leg love
Is like aloha.
It says hello and goodbye.
It says welcome home
And don't leave.
Not always in that order.
Not just are you
Going to feed me now?
The figure eight dance
Around and through your legs
Is familiar love.
Purrs and all,
You wouldn't have it
Any other way.
At the start of your morning
Or at the end of your day.
Until there's a lap for sitting
The game's always the same.
Leg love belongs to your cat.
It's part of their game
And you wouldn't have it
Any other way...
The day just wouldn't be the same.

A Brand New Day

No matter how careful
We try to be,
No matter how safe
We think we are,
There are just some things
We can never see coming.
An accident, a mistake, an error
That ends up in a disaster
That can change our lives forever.
But when a blessing comes along
We relish the joy it brings us everyday.
Forgetting sometimes that the same thing
That brought the blessing into our lives
Can take it away from us at any time.
Without making any sense in the moment and
For no reason at all
We can never know when that may be.
We forget sometimes
In our everyday lives that our dogs
And cats are only on loan to us.
That this joy that completely fills our hearts
With their unconditional love
Will one day be gone.
We close our eyes in the fountain
Of love they shower on us every day
Only to be suddenly jolted wake
By a tragedy, accident or misfortune
That stop the hands of time.
To find ourselves stunned, lost at sea.
Forgetting what land even looks like

Or where it might even be.
Adrift in our anger, loss, and despair.
That's when we need to keep the faith the most.
And know when we come back to shore
Our lives will be forever changed
And different than before.
Accidents will happen
And mistakes will be made,
And that no one is to blame.
No more than the fire for its flame,
The thunder for its lightning,
The cloud for its rain.
Though fires may come and burn us down,
Lightning strike us dead
And floods wash our lives away,
Tomorrow will always come.
And with it brings a brand new day.
With each blessing that leaves us
Through our window,
A new one is patiently waiting
At our door.
To help us find our way again.
Until we're ready
After we're healed
To open our hearts and let it in.

Without Dog

Once you've found dog,
Had dog, loved and been loved by dog,
It's hard to go back
To a life without dog.
Your heart has been stretched
To it's limits by unconditional love.
And it never regains its original shape.
Its capacity and volume
To hold love for everything has grown.
So, without dog
Something seems to be missing.
Your heart never seems to be
Quite as full and running over
As it was before,
When there was life with dog.
A walk is just a walk.
It may take you where you're going
But you might miss something,
That dog made sure you stopped to see.
The little things along the way.
Without dog it's easy
To get lost in only the purpose
Of your walk, out and back.
In getting from here to there.
And miss the joy of being with someone
Who is nothing short of love itself.
From the ground up.
Who only wants to be with you
For whatever reason
Whenever you go.

Where ever you go.
Without dog
There's a loneliness of only purpose
In everyday life.
Without dog to point out
The joys of life itself to us, in the journey
And all the love that exists in between...
In just being alive.
Without dog
Life can be rather lonely sometimes
Without someone to share it with.
Take time to really see life itself.
To touch it.
To smell it.
To taste it and hear it.
Dog is the unconditional love
At the end of the leash
That slows us down in our days
Just enough to notice those little things
We might have otherwise missed
On our journey to get
From here to there,
From day to day.
Then comfort us in our evenings

As we go off to sleep.
It's only after they're gone
We realize that without dog
Our walks seem to lack the joy in their purpose.
In something that isn't just being about us
And takes us outside of ourselves
With a love that is immeasurable.
Something that has become so familiar
In its routine that we may not notice
Its true value until its gone.
When we're walking, without dog
Without a leash, silently for whatever reason
Alone, with only our purpose
That's when we really notice how much
We truly miss our dearest friend.
Who loved us in spite of ourselves
For all the right reasons.
With love and joy at the end of our leash.
Love on demand. Loyal and true.
Until their last day
Whose only thought was
To spend their time with you.
Going with us where ever we go
Hanging on our every word.

Eating with us. Sleeping with us.
Never missing a chance to be in our arms.
And always ready for a kiss.
Love without limits, on demand, 24/7.

There's freedom
To life without dog.
To be alone, and sometimes lonely too.
Free and untethered by the responsibilities
Of life with dog...
To come and go as you please.
To be free to have only yourself
To think about. To be responsible for.
To be alone.
With your thoughts, your loves, your joys
And the pain you feel
When your wrap your arms around yourself
And hold onto your life with empty arms
Where your one true friend use to be.
The warm spot in your heart
That doesn't leave a shadow anymore.
Where the love that stretched your heart
To its limits, from beginning to end
Has left a wrinkle
Where your best friend use to be.
Has been.

A warm spot where the sun once shown
And shines again in every dog you see,
In every dog you meet.
And reminds you as long as your alive
That the sun will shine again.
And take all the wrinkles out of your heart
When you open your arms
To let your next dog in.
Don't wait too long
For that hole to close, it never does.
All your dogs are with you
From beginning to end.
Don't wait too long
To let the love back in
And take the wrinkles out of your heart.
Without dog
We learn the true meaning
Of man's best friend.
That a walk is just a walk
Without dog.
Without joy in our purpose,
Without dog
A walk is just a walk
Out and back again....

Run To Me

Run to me
You wild creatures
In all your reckless abandon.
Like birds in flight
Your loving hearts bursting open,
Your eyes flashing wide and bright.
Pouring all your intentions in my direction
Your feet barely hitting the ground.

Run to me
Oh heart of my hearts.
I've loved you both
Right from the start.
The moment I saw you,
You became a part of me.

Bring me all of your love
As fast as you can run—
Unbridled, unshod, and free.
And I'll be the one
With arms wide open
For you to run to me.

No greater joy
In all of God's creatures
Have I found in Mother Nature
With all your loving dog gone features
Has touched my soul
Like you...

Run to me.
Run to me.
Run to me.

With your wild eyes and racing hearts
And I'll be there to welcome you
With open arms into mine.
It's something I love to watch you do
When you run to me,
Time, after time, after time.

All Things Left Behind

I was fussin' around out in my office
The other day (the garage)
Looking for something
I know I put away but couldn't find.
It was just a rake but I'd it had for years
Kept echoing in my mind.
I know I was right
This wasn't a mistake.
So I opened a beer
And tried to remember again
When it all became clear
From the back of my mind.
My rake had become a victim
Of all things left behind.
There were times in my life
When I was more settled down
And I stayed in one place for a while.
Sometimes I was married and others I was not,
And I slowly began to smile.
Remembering that I moved
To keep from losing my mind
And that's when things would go missing...
Falling into the black whole of
All things left behind.
So after a couple more beers
I tried to recall some things
Gone missing over the years,
And where I'd dropped or left the ball.
I had moved so many times lately
I've forgotten how to remember

Where I put some things
Or if I even had them at all.
It's funny what we chose
To take with us when we go
So we'll have it for the next place we find.
But sometimes no matter how hard we try
We may not need something so
Something's get left behind.
Tools and clothes and stereos
Leave a comet trail across the years
And fond memories
Of what's lost in my mind,
But that was then and this is now
And that doesn't help me find....
The rake, the clippers, my favorite boots that
Have all vanished and yet somehow
Have been replaced with a newer kind.
The same will go for me one day,
Which makes it easier for me to let go
Of the things that are holding me back.
You know all those things I can't seem to find?
The eye of the needle is only so big;
You only need the clothes on your back.
But that will be then and this is now

And I still need some of that.
I'm sure it was here yesterday
When it finally crosses my mind....
Yesterday was two years ago.
Some things I don't even know are missing yet!
No wonder there is nothing here to find.
They're probably in a pile somewhere, I'll bet...
Of all things left behind....

So Many People

So many people out there
Are walking around talking around
To themselves right now more and more these days.
Makes it hard to tell
Who the nut jobs really are!
There's voice activated hands-free, and Bluetooth too!
So while you're driving around in your car
You can talk to someone if you absolutely have to,
And I think you all know who those people are.
So I just throw a pair of earbuds on and
Start talking to myself going off around the bend.
When I slipped off bar and slid sideways
Down under myself again.

There's psychotics, neurotics, and bi-polars too!
Walking and talking to themselves
All around you.
It's really quite a test these days
To sort 'em all out and see
Who the crazy ones really are;
I just hope that it's you and not me!

With my ear buds in I can talk all day
I can scream and shout while I'm walking about
And people think I'm just singing along,
Walking and rocking to some punk rock band,
Boy Howdy! Have they got that wrong...

So many people are talking to people
When there's nobody standing there,
Only nobody seems to notices anymore
And nobody seems to care.
But it all works out for me in the end.
I just plug myself in and start talking again
To myself all I want everywhere!

The Locker Room

In the locker room
There is no mercy.
Everyone sees things just as they are.
Sagging skin, bulging muscles,
Hair or not,
Where it shouldn't be,
Where it use to be.
Every wrinkle, every scar
Has a story.
Young and old,
All different, all the same
Versions of God's perfect machine.
In the locker room
All pretenses are dropped
When your towel hits the floor
And there's nothing between you
And the light of the naked truth.
Everyone's looking
And nobody cares, but you.
We're all God's children
In God's view.
The locker room is just a test.
We're all the same in different ways.
No one's better or worse
Than the rest.
Only God knows the whole truth.
All we can do is be our best.

Last Night's Clothes

When last nights clothes
Become your morning clothes
Just because they're there, on the bed post
You realize something...
You're older now, a lot older,
And you don't let these little things
Bother you as much as you use too.
Your clothes aren't dirty
And they're still good for a few more hours
Before you shower, but you still hope no one sees you
In yesterdays clothes in the early morning hours.
Because what matters most right now
Is the dogs have to go out.
Don't worry about your hair,
You put on your morning hat, grab the paper and
Let in the cat.
Start the coffee and have a piece of toast.
It's the start of another day.
Everyone's up and you feel okay.
Everything's working
In a human and animal sort of way
So let the love begin.
My life is blessed. No wait...
Always has been all these years.
Equal parts laughter and joy
Mixed in with a little tragedy and tears,
That's the way life is.
The bad times seem to go so slow and last
Too long while you're in them,
And the good times?

They always seem to go by too fast.
Too soon they fall into memories
And become the past.
Children come and grandparents go,
Not always in that order
And in the twinkling of an eye.
One moment we're saying hello
To a brand new world we don't know
And the next moment:
"Someone else is dressing us and taking us
Where we do not want to go". John 21:18
And we're saying goodbye.
Makes wearing yesterdays clothes seem
Pretty irrelevant with a cat in your lap
While you read the paper,
And a hot cup of coffee on the arm of your favorite chair
As you count your blessings one by one
And head into a new day.
Trying to be a better person
Than the one you were the day before.
And give thanks to the Lord
That you even got one more day

Phil Pochurek

To be alive and live, one more day
To live and give someone a piece of your heart.
The same way Jesus gave His
To all of us, back from the start.
Breathe life in and drink it all up
Before it goes...
Then finish your coffee in last night's clothes.

He Sings In Tongues

He sings in tongues.
Melody? Sometimes.
Chorus? Always and in unison.
Like banging pots and pans hanging from a tree
Blowing in the wind.
Broken glass popping and snapping
Across a hot plate skillet
Over an open flame.
Shouting jibber jabber!
Picture Robert De Niro in Cape Fear.
Going down with the ship.
Jim Carey trying to lie
In Liar Liar.
Or Robin Williams doing stand up
Like Mork at lightning speed.
Full-throttled open voice
In the open privacy of his moving car.
He sings in tongues
Full-throated for the pure joy
Of the tone, the vibration, a sound
Ground into raw vowels disassembled
And reassembled for his listening pleasure.
In a language only he knows,
To a tune only he hears,
A song sang in tongues
Meant only for his ears.

Phil Pochurek

Ashes To Ashes Dust To Dust

We all began in much the same way.
In a drop of rain, in a flake of snow
Molded and shaped from a hand full of clay.
There's a rhythm, a sound inside us
In everything we do.
Breathe in breathe out, breathe in breathe out,
From God to us from me to you
Is pretty much what life is all about.
I've seen the light up in the sky
And the fire on the ground.
We live our lives somewhere in between...
Somewhere there's a meaning to be found.
In our youth the wind is in our face.
We're always running somewhere.
Never knowing, never caring what lies ahead.
At times it seems like we're running in place.
We're indestructible, immortal, and impatient.
Our virtues only beginning to line up.
Until that moment, a tipping point in time
When the wind shifts and moves behind us
Full on our backs.
And we can feel our mortality
Breathing down our necks.
So we dig our heels in
As it blows us from our comfort zone—
The warm familiarity of the present,
The land of the living
Towards our inevitable fate.
Down an unknown path that lies ahead.
A grandchild is born.

A parent or sibling passes
And someone you know has cancer...
With eyes wide open
We lean back into the winds of fate
And choose our steps with care.
Every heartbeat reminds us they have a number
And every breath is precious.
We eat more slowly
We choose our words with care
And listen more carefully to the world around us,
Love is all that matters.
We race as humans
All towards the same end
Our faith in God we trust...
All back to the beginning
To do it all again.
Ashes to ashes and dust to dust.

Two Words

Walking along with my head
Bowed low in full meditation,
Looking down as I go
Unaware of my direction,
The dogs know the way.
I wonder now the longer I live
Which one is harder?
To be obedient or to forgive.
On my journey down the road
To the truth.
Obedience and forgiveness.
Two words I never considered
In my youth,
Now I think about them everyday.
The longer I live the more I know
But the harder it gets
For me to let go
Of my heart, my mind,
When it's all I have left to show
For the life I've lived,
And I need them to help me find
My way home.
Obedience keeps me from losing my mind
And forgiveness heals and helps me find
My heart along the way.
Without them I would be lost.
Had I only known them in my youth
I wouldn't have paid such a high price
And suffered what it cost...
To know the truth.

With Heads Bowed Low

With heads bowed low
No ones looking up anymore,
With their hearts,
Their minds, or their eyes.
It's no wonder no one knows
Where they're going.
Lost in their screens,
Looking for answers and playing games,
It's no surprise everyone's
Become so all knowing.
We're constantly taking pictures
Of ourselves and our food.
In case we might forget
Who we are or what we ate
That we haven't noticed yet, we're getting lost.
Trying our best to get ahead or win
And not be late,
No one's noticed what it cost.

Somewhere down the pathway through mankind
With a handful of digital seeds
We planted the tree of technology,
Which helped us in the beginning
Save time and fulfill our needs,
But somewhere along the path
We lost our way...
And the digital tree of knowledge grew.
Now everyone has a digital apple
In their hands from that tree
And we've all seem to have forgotten

Everything we ever knew.
Instead of when asking questions
About something we want to know
Then looking up for ourselves to see—
We're playing games, taking pictures of our food
Then turning our camera's on us
And shouting to the world
"Hey look at me."

We use to reach out to others
To give a helping hand.
Now we put our apples
On the end of a stick and shout
"Look at me I'm the greatest in the land."
And it all started with one byte.
The flavor of this knowledge
Soon created quite a demand
To satisfy our desires,
With the cries for more apples
And room for more bytes we
Grew more desperate and loud
While the digital tree reached for the sky.
Bursting with knowledge in a flash of light
It gave birth to the digital cloud.

Where everyone can shout and be
A star in their own digital sky:
"There is no God, but look at me.
I'm here now and this is what I do!
Don't you all wish that you could be me
Right now instead of you?"

Everyone holds an apple now
That fell from that digital tree.
It's part of who we all are.
So no one asks how anymore:
How we could come so far,
With our heads bowed low
Without looking up to see where we are
Or where we should go.
With heads bowed low we pray to a god
Who lives in a digital cloud.
Asking questions from our most recent desires.
Hoping for answers to quench our thirst
For our latest cravings...
Only to create more fires.
By now we should have learned.
When you pray with your thumbs
Instead of your heart

You could end up getting burned
From a god who doesn't exist.
Stubborn in our pursuit of glory
We take another selfie and persist.
Without shame we eat from this tree
And it's apple we hold in our hand.
Eating taking kilobytes and gigabytes as
We bow our heads across the land.
Asking questions from a god who doesn't exist.
Storing our answers in a digital cloud.
Next to all the pictures we've taken of ourselves
And all the dinners we've had.
Looking for happiness in the palm of our hands
That can't be found, how truly sad,
Instead of looking up to the Lord.
And yet we still persist...
With heads bowed low and an apple in our hand
We pray with our thumbs on a digital screen
To a god who doesn't exist.
With our heads bowed low
And an apple in our hands
We still persist.

A New Golden Calf

A light mist fell through the veil of a cloud
As it settled over the gathering below.
It was a familiar shroud... in Moses's day
Shuttering out the blue sky, overhead.
Silencing its natural beauty in a Godly way
To see if anyone would look up instead.
We use to raise our arms
To the heavens and ask why
When we didn't know the answers for ourselves.
Raise our hands to pray.
Now we bow our heads
And pray with our thumbs
To a new Golden Calf,
That's in everyone's pocket today.
One we can hold in our hand.
No need for the sky
When we ask why to a digital god
As we bow our heads and say:
"Tell me what I want to know."
"What I should say?"
"How do I get to where I need to go."
"What should I believe in today?"
A silicone god that's always there
As long as you have a charge
With an answer for anything
You could ever ask;
Its knowledge is omnisciently large.
Its speed is the new light,
So certainly it must be true.
If it's on the Internet where everything

Is right in front of you.
A digital god I can hold in my hand
Who's never let me down.
Who answers whenever I call.
Who's always there when I need them to be
Yet not anywhere at all.
Off in a cloud I can hold in my hand
Where all good gods should be.
No wonder it's always raining
Down tears from the sky.
No one looks up for answers anymore
To ask their questions why.
We bow our heads
And pray with our thumbs
To get everything we need.
We get our answers by looking down.
No more soil of faith in the hearts of men
To grow our mustard seeds.
We count our wealth in gigabytes now
It's the only memory we need.

It only took us a few hundred years
To surrender our souls to mankind.
How soon we've forgotten our Lord.
We pray with our thumbs now

To pocket prophets in the palms of our hands,
And no one ever gets bored.
Tapping out questions we use to ask Jesus
In an endless series of questions and demands...
Shamelessly we hide now in plain sight,
Pretending no one sees us.
Our god is conveniently stored in the cloud
Without worries where our souls are going,
While the devil patiently waits to reap
The seeds that he's been sewing.
His Golden Calf is never wrong.
As we bow our heads with pride
And pray with our thumbs
By proclaiming how right we are
In all the glory of our unknowing...
We bow our heads and pray with our thumbs
Not looking at where we're going.
With our new Golden Calf
In the palm of our hands
We pray to the Google, all knowing.

At 4:45

Every morning at 4:45
His routine is always the same.
With a coffee cup in one hand
And his Bible in the other he's ready to begin
To receive God's graces in Jesus's name.
Reading them by the fireside
Over and over again.
The dogs are sleeping quietly on their beds
There's a cat curled up on his lap
While he reads to the rising sun,
As the Lord pours His love into his heart
Every morning until his reading is done.
With grace and wisdom unmatched in men
From a well that never runs dry
His words ring out loud and clear,
With love and forgiveness as time goes by
For the short time that we're here.
He reads God's word over and over
At the beginning of everyday
To remind him where he came from
And to help him along his way.
Then reads them again every evening
At the end of another day.
Giving thanks to the Lord above
For all His graces He's shared with him
And for filling him with his love.
Then he rests his head upon his pillow
And his heart in Jesus's hands,
Who was blameless without sin,
Until 4:45 and a brand new sunrise
When he wakes up to praise God again.

Amen

Phil Pochurek

In Every Soul We See

I realize now that some doing
Must be done, always be done
Before there is some being,
Who we can become.
The one who God meant for us to be.
Over time and down the road
We must learn to listen up and see;
Learn how to carry our load
Before we can become, can be
The best version of ourselves
That God want's us to be.
The best version of yourself
That no one else can be but you.
Just as I can't be someone else
Instead of me.
Lord knows I've tried to.
That's the reason we all know
Why Jesus died....

The Old Ones

The old ones
Come to the study
To huddle around the Word.
Not because of what they know
Or how long they've been around,
But because of all the things they've seen
and heard.
For some it glows like a fire
Giving off heat and light.
For others it's a wellspring of clean water
Quenching their thirst for what's good and right.

Like old growth trees
Whose roots run deep
Into ancient soils of the past,
They're anchored by old familiar ways.
Making it easy to get lost
In the shadows they cast
Even on cloudy days...

And when they leave
Some will take fire
From the burning bush,
And some will take water
From the living well.

Take fire in a torch
For light, for heat, for the ovens
To bake their unleavened bread.
To eat and be consumed by the Word
Like the old ones gone before, long dead.

Take water in a pail
In a cup, to drink, to wash
To swim in the sea of His love.
In the living water of His Word
From below as above.

The old ones
Come to the study
To huddle around the Word...
To share in the glory
Of the greatest words ever spoken
That anyone has ever heard.

When The Devil Comes To Dinner

When the devil comes to dinner
He sits down with a smile.
There's fire in his eyes
When he politely asks
If he may stay for a while.
No one knows where he came from
Or who he really is.
With his finger on the trigger
Under the table
Your fate has now become his.
He speaks in softened colors,
His words alive and bright,
No one has the slightest idea
That this would be their last night.
When the last seat is finally taken
He says "lets bow our heads in prayer."
Then slowly he takes the safety off
And rises up out of his chair.
He fires at the first one who looks up,
Then quickly one by one,
He dispatches the rest as they sit there
Before they can get up and run.
And when the room is finally empty,
But for the screams and hysterical tears,
He looks at what he has done.
Everyone at the table is dead...
He smiles, one bullet left in his gun.
The tablecloth is dripping red.

No need for him to hurry
Or even try to escape
As he raises the gun to his head.
He knows where he is going,
The bullet is the key to his gate.
Who knows where the devil comes from
His address is written in hate.
Too often we welcome him with open arms
Then realize it too late.
Make sure whenever you come to a table
To sit with your friends and break bread
You give thanks to the Lord
For what you're about to receive.
Because one of them may be the devil
And take your soul with him
When he leaves.

The Wings Around Your Heart

Walking, walking, walking,
I think I'm finally starting to figure it out.
Life that is with all its trials
And what it's all about.
Why sometimes when I'm walking
I can feel something loose inside
Like a peanut when it rattles in its shell.
Something is changing inside of me
And I can feel it, I can tell
That it's almost ready.
We all have a soul inside of us
Like a caterpillar in a cocoon,
Waiting and growing the whole of our lives
Trying not to come out too soon.
Sometimes I feel it more than others
Loose inside me just under the skin
And other days I feel it clear to the bone.
Growing in spurts depending on
If I use it or leave it alone.
Now the older I get
The more I'm aware of it
As my body breaks down, wears out, and falls apart;
What that rattle is inside my chest and
That it's nothing for me to worry about.
It's just the sound the wings are making
That are growing around my heart.

Our body is the chrysalis, the temple
That keeps our soul alive,
And depending on how well we take care of it
Will determine if it will survive.
To live long enough to grow its wings
So when we die it can carry our heart
Back to the beginning, to the source, our Lord
The maker of all things from the start.
And when our bodies wear out and slip away...
We'll all be knowing where our souls will be going
On that fateful day.
When they take wing and fly back to Him...
With our one and only heart.

Phil Pochurek

Everyone Has A Story

In the beginning we head down the road,
Our windshields clean and clear.
Off on the road trip of our lives
To find out why we're here.
In our youth our pedal is to the metal;
Fearlessly we drive into the night.
Hoping to find what we're looking for,
Trying to do what's right.
Stopping we only deceive ourselves
Then check our mirrors for a little hindsight.
Give someone a helping hand
Here and there,
See if our tires need any air
And satisfy a few of our desires...
Help someone get a foot up in life,
Maybe put out a few fires.
But the road is long no end in sight,
As we begin to rack up the miles.
Everyone has a story to tell
Hidden behind their smiles.
Some are full of drama and tragedy,
Others of faith and glory.
Just under the surface
Or buried deep inside
Everyone has a story.
No matter how hard you try to escape
Don't let them hold you back,
For some too much is never enough,
For others life's an empty sack.
Whatever story your life becomes

Wherever your road may take you
Our stories aren't for everyone,
But there's One who won't forsake you.
Every story ever told
All go down in the same book.
All subject to the same review.
Written first on every heart
In the deepest part of you.
It's up to you to find your way...or not
And let your story do the telling—
In the end it's all you've got.
Your chapter in the Book of Life
Depends on how long you live,
Not on whether you won or lost
But what you had to give.

www.ingramcontent.com/pod-product-compliance
Lightning Source LLC
LaVergne TN
LVHW091548060526
838200LV00036B/755